This is a work of fiction. Similarities to real people, places, or events are entirely coincidental.

THE BEAST GETS HIS COWGIRL

First edition. July 2, 2020.

Copyright © 2020 Jessie Gussman.

Written by Jessie Gussman.

Cover art by Brenda Walter
Editing by Heather Hayden
Narration by Jay Dyess

Acknowledgements: Writing a heroine who had been born and raised in the UK was intimidating to me. I would like to thank Nicola Pepper, a reader and friend – who happens to share my birthday – from London, for taking a look at my manuscript and giving me a hand with Madeline – her thoughts and speech. We did our best to accurately portray the speech patterns of someone who had been born and raised in the UK, but who had spent the last twelve years in America. Her help was invaluable and selfless.

All errors and mistakes are my own, of course.

~Jessie

Chapter 1

"And... Roll!"

The red taping light came on, and Madeline flashed a smile that showcased both deep dimples in her cheeks. It was part of what had made her famous. Those dimples.

That, and her mossy green eyes.

Well, and her classic features, which she got from her mother.

Her childhood in the UK was a long time ago and felt far away as she stood in the kitchen studio in the middle of Hollywood with a giant NFL football player in front of her. She couldn't remember his name. Jarvis? Jarnell? Something with a J. No, wait, the J was last week. Or the week before.

Bollocks, she should at least remember the guy's name.

"Khalil." A quiet voice came in her earpiece. Cheryl, bless her sweet heart. Madeline had no idea what she'd do without her best friend who happened to hail from Australia.

Making a mental note to thank her later, she looked up at the giant beside her. "So now, Khalil, you know what we're doing next, right?"

She pulled her cheeks in tighter to really make her dimples jump. She was an expert at it. It was necessary to distract from the fact that, while she was a world-famous chef, with five best-selling cookbooks out, and an even better selling children's cookbook, and two cooking shows, she didn't, in fact, have the slightest idea of how to cook.

She could barely boil water.

She was forever grateful for Cheryl.

Few people could resist her dimples, and Khalil wasn't one of them. He gave her a killer smile, not anything that helped him be successful on the field in the NFL, but it probably was a huge boon to him off the field. Maybe if they'd been sitting at a bar together, that smile would've made her own grow real.

But they weren't at a bar, they were in front of the cameras on her cooking show, and she had to be on *her* game.

"I think it's gotta be time to eat." Khalil clapped his teeth together, not the first time he'd done it during taping, and Madeline had almost grown used to it. She didn't even blink that time. She'd met all kinds on her show, honestly, but this was the first teeth clacker.

"Not quite. A good meal takes time and patience." Her British accent made her words ring with authority. Or at least that's what people told her when they watched her show. She hoped so. Her accent was another one of those buffers, like her smile, her dimples, and her facial features that she put out there to take people's attention off the one thing that could make her entire kingdom of cards come crashing down.

"Take the tomatoes and pour them over the top of the chicken in the slow cooker." Cheryl's voice came softly in her earpiece.

Madeline's hand reached out for the bowl with the red things in them.

"No! Not the red peppers. The tomatoes. Next bowl over."

Cheryl always had her back. Thankfully. She didn't know why it was so hard for her to tell vegetables apart, although she did know why she'd never been able to learn how to cook.

Well, she didn't actually know. It had something to do with her artist brain and the fact that she couldn't concentrate for more than three seconds at a time. That made her good at seeing the next business opportunity and always staying on top of trends, but it made it really hard for her to learn anything that took more than a glance or that – even worse – actually had steps to it. It was a miracle, and a testament to her mother's determination, that she could even read.

"We're going to put these tomatoes with green chilis over the top of the chicken in the slow cooker. Would you like to do the honors, Khalil?" She added batting eyes to her flashing dimples.

Khalil held out his hand and took the bowl. "Like this?" He held the bowl over the chicken in the slow cooker, waiting to pour until she gave the okay.

"Yes. Just like that," Cheryl's voice spoke into her earbud.

"Yes. Just like that," Madeline echoed.

She watched as the big man carefully poured the tomatoes over the chicken, never getting over the fact that she had her own cooking show and had no bloody clue what to do next.

"The bacon! The bacon in the oven! You better get that out, or it's going to burn."

"The bacon!" she exclaimed, startling Khalil, who dumped the last half of the tomatoes out in a blob rather than sprinkling them over the chicken like he'd been doing.

Madeline didn't apologize. That was part of the appeal of her show. It looked so spontaneous, and she seemed so surprised when the next step needed to happen. That's because she truly *was* surprised. But her audience just loved her quirkiness, and her cooking show had shot to number one, easily beating all the other cooking shows on TV.

"Would you like to get the bacon out?" Madeline asked, a little breathlessly, because it wouldn't do for the stuff to burn. It had been a question, but moot, since she was already handing the oven mitts to Khalil and not giving him a choice.

That was another problem. She was afraid of the oven. It was hot, obviously, and she never failed to scorch her eyeballs when she opened the door, no matter how hard she concentrated. So far, her eyebrows had escaped mostly unscathed, although she had needed an eyebrow pencil to fill her left one in for about four months last summer after Cheryl hadn't noticed she'd closed the door while broiling steak. That was the last time she'd touched an oven.

Less dangerously, she had no clue how to set the timer. Which was why she depended on Cheryl to let her know when things were done.

"Make sure he's careful with the grease," Cheryl said in her earbud.

"Grease is hot. Keep it in the pot," Madeline said.

Khalil's eyes lifted to hers, a bit of humor in them, before he continued to bend over, both lips sucked in and biting down hard. Madeline would almost laugh, because he looked like this was his first time getting anything out of the oven, except she knew she would look the exact same way, only worse, because just like the big football player—was he a linebacker? A defensive back? She had no clue and couldn't care less. She certainly didn't follow American football. It was way too smash-mouth and violent for her – give her a good game of polo any day – and she had never gotten used to it, even if she had been in the country for over a decade.

But she could relate—she would have fear on her face too.

How she'd managed to do a cooking show without opening the oven even one single time in the last six months was a feat that should have earned her an actual acting award. But if that were ever to happen, people would have to know that she'd been faking it these last two years.

Khalil was able to get the bacon out of the oven and set it on the counter.

"Hand him the tongs, and tell him to put the bacon over the top of the chicken in the cooker."

Madeline did as Cheryl commanded, adding her own spin of quirk to it that had the audience laughing and Khalil giving her that smile which had several ladies in the small live audience throwing phone numbers at security.

While she was doing that, Cheryl continued, "Now explain to the audience that you're cooking the bacon, the chicken, and the tomatoes together for six hours because it will add flavor to the meat."

Madeline fluttered her eyelashes. "Normally, people don't cook their bacon with their chicken, because they like it to be crispy. They put it on at the end. But we want all those yummy, delicious, salty-flavored good tastes out of the bacon and into our chicken. That's why we put it in before we cook the chicken."

That was another thing she was good at, totally making things up. Cheryl could give her the bare bones, and she could make it into something outrageous and outlandish. Again, her audience considered her quirky and loved every second of it. That's what made her cookbooks successful. Cheryl came up with the recipes and the directions, of course, and Madeline added the flare and dash that made it unique.

"Think the bacon would just be good if we ate it now," Khalil said.

"Me too. Let's save two pieces back." Madeline didn't bother with the tongs. She just grabbed two pieces off the tray. "Oh, these are hot." She tossed them back and forth between her hands.

"They just came out of the oven," Khalil said.

Madeline managed to not have a retort for that. She honestly didn't expect any football player that cooked with her to add much to the conversation about food other than eating it. Not that she subscribed to the stereotype of dumb jocks necessarily, but Cheryl was in charge of booking them, and she wouldn't book someone who was going to be able to figure out that Madeline wasn't what the entire world believed she was.

She tossed the bacon around until she felt it was cool enough to put in her mouth.

"Oh yeah, this is good stuff. Here." She handed the other piece to Khalil, who set the tongs down and took the bacon, putting the whole thing in his mouth at once before picking up the tongs again.

"Handy. To have a mouth big enough that it can hold an entire piece of bacon."

Khalil grinned at her. "It makes everything better."

It sure did.

THE BEAST GETS HIS COWGIRL IN THE SHOW ME STATE 7

Cheryl's voice came through her earbud. "Have him put the lid on and turn it on low and tell everyone that it needs to cook for six hours." There was relief in her tone. Every single show they taped, they ran the risk of their scheme being exposed.

"Grab the lid and put those babies to bed. In six short hours, you'll have a meal your mum will be proud of."

Khalil was a sweet guy, and, like most of the football players she had on her show, when she mentioned his mum, his smile got huge. He looked in the camera, waved, and mouthed a "Hi, Mom."

She just loved it when they did that. So adorable.

"Now it's time for you to get the chicken out of the warmer and put some on two plates for you guys."

She had Khalil do that, relief making her a little giddy. Giddier than usual anyway. The folks at home were used to it and expected it from her show.

Brits were supposed to have a stiff upper lip and be maybe a little stuffy, but while she had the accent, she totally missed the personality. It was all because of her dad, who had been half Italian, half French and could never resist a good time. Which was probably the reason he only stayed with her mum long enough to conceive a child and not long enough to raise it. Madeline had never even met him.

She only knew him through her mum's stories, which always seemed sad at the end, like her mother would have gone with him if she hadn't been tied down with a baby to raise.

Maybe that gave her daddy issues. Maybe that's why she sought the limelight and what had started out as a YouTube sensation with Cheryl sitting on the floor behind the counter telling her what to do while Madeline stood and flashed a grin while putting together whatever recipe Cheryl would come up with.

Their quirky popularity had eventually landed them a contract and a ride to Hollywood.

She and Khalil both took a bite of the chicken on their plates, declared it good, and smiled at each other.

She mentioned the special guest in a hook for the next show, then Stella, the director, called, "That's a wrap."

Another one in the books and still not outed.

"Thanks for being such a great sport, Khalil. And for coming on the show," Madeline said, holding out her hand. Khalil switched his fork to his left hand and grabbed her right.

"This stuff is actually pretty good. It didn't even seem that hard to make. I think I could do it. Can I take the rest of this home and maybe that stuff in the crockpot, too?"

She often sent the leftovers home with guests or stagehands. Whoever wanted it. Whatever was left went to homeless shelters. "I'll make sure that you get all that we have, and I'll have the staff get you a printed and autographed recipe."

"Thanks," he said, his fist out.

She bumped his fist, and they grinned at each other.

"I thought this would be boring, but you're kinda cute. What're you doing Friday night?"

"She's busy," Stella said as she walked out and put her arm around Madeline. "And she's leaving now. She and I have to talk about the new show that's in development and just had the schedule moved up on it."

Madeline's heart stalled and seemed to hang suspended in her chest for long moments as her stomach gesticulated in ways that had nothing to do with the food that was in it.

She swallowed, and her voice came out harsher than what she'd expected. "They moved the schedule up? By how much?"

"They want to start filming in two weeks."

Unconsciously, Madeline's hand went to her middle, and her mouth hung open. What was she going to do?

Thankfully, Cheryl came stepping down from the overhead room from which she always watched. It gave her a better view and helped her to see exactly what Madeline needed at all times.

But her mother had been ill, and after they taped the next and last show of the season, she was headed back to Australia to spend two months with her. She'd already put the trip off once and had been very clear about the fact that she did not want to do it again.

"I'm not sure that's going to work," Madeline said, trying to project confidence into her voice and British upper-crust manner. It was all she had, because she had no excuse not to start filming in two weeks. Just because Cheryl wasn't going to be there, no one would think that she would turn it down.

"I'm afraid we don't have a choice. The decision was made three days ago, and they have already put a ton of advertising money into it. They assumed it would be okay with you, since originally, you had committed to working with a local LA charity for the next two months. We just flip-flop those dates. I've already taken care of it for you."

"You did a great job, honey," Cheryl said, gliding in and giving her a hug. "What's wrong?" Her brows furrowed in concern as she looked between Madeline and Stella. Cheryl knew her better than anyone and had obviously picked up on her internal panic.

"Maybe there was something bad in that bacon." Stella shook her head. "I can't believe you guys just took two pieces of bacon and ate them. Right in front of the camera. Your shows are just crazy."

Madeline pulled her lips back, but she knew that the expression on her face couldn't even begin to be termed a smile. She felt like her entire torso was bubbling like the inside of a volcano.

"Madeline?" Cheryl asked.

By now, Madeline no longer had her breathing under control, and she was panting like a dog on the sidewalk in the middle of summer. At least her tongue wasn't hanging out. That she knew of. She almost put a hand up to check. She felt like she was floating and physically out of touch with everything that was going on around her.

"They want to move *Cooking in the Country* up. They want to start filming in two weeks. They've already started advertising it." She felt like she was saying each line breathlessly and fatalistically. It was like nails in her coffin. There was no way she could do this without Cheryl. No way.

But as much as she wanted to beg her friend, drop to her knees right now and plead with her friend, she couldn't. Cheryl had been putting off seeing her mother for a while. And Madeline could not live with herself if her mother died before Cheryl got to see her one last time. She couldn't take that away from her friend. Not even to save their cooking empire.

Cheryl immediately grasped the implications, as Madeline knew she would, and her blue eyes clouded and narrowed in concern while compassion filled her face.

"Maybe I could put off my trip?" she said softly and slowly, hesitantly, like she was afraid that Madeline would say *yes, please do*.

But Madeline couldn't be that selfish. She wanted to be, and it was on the tip of her tongue to be, but she couldn't ask her friend to give up visiting her cancer-ridden mother. She straightened her back, even though she knew she wouldn't be fooling Cheryl, but she could put on a good front.

"No. Don't you change a thing. You will be on a plane three days from now, and you will be seeing your mum not long after that. I won't have it any other way."

"Cheryl is always around to hold your hand, but it looks like you're going to have to start doing some things on your own." Stella tapped a few things on her iPad and then tucked it under her arm. "I'll send you the details as soon as I have them. I believe Chandler Hudson has his brother in Missouri talked into allowing us to use his place. He lives on a real farm and actually works it, but also happens to have a world-class kitchen because his hobby is cooking. We scored big time with that, and this show is going to be a smashing success. You'll just have to adjust a few plans." Stella raised her eyebrows and pressed her lips together. She was used to dealing with diva moments, although typically not from Madeline.

Madeline was far more likely to be off dreaming up a new idea or goofing off in the break room or hanging out with any kids that were brought to the set that day than she was to be having a diva moment.

But, no doubt, right now, make no mistake, she was definitely having a major diva moment. Only she had to pretend she wasn't, or at least she had to keep the real reason for the diva surfacing under wraps.

Stella walked away, leaving Cheryl and Madeline alone in the corner.

"That really threw a spanner in the works." Madeline tried not to look too awful. She was not going to guilt Cheryl into staying.

"I really can cancel my trip if it will help you."

She would. The Empire was theirs, not just Madeline's, and Madeline didn't forget it for one moment. They split everything equally, even though Madeline was the face.

Cheryl had never tried to take center stage. First of all, Cheryl freely admitted she didn't have the looks to be in front of the camera. Which was sad, since the person with the talent should be rewarded with the contract, but they'd known from the start things would never be that way.

Cheryl had been fine with it. She was self-conscious about her looks and hated to be photographed, let alone videoed. She was also quite humble, perfectly content to let Madeline be the face of everything, happy to be able to spend all of her time creating recipes the entire world could love and that Madeline could put her quirky personality into and earn them both a comfortable paycheck.

"No. Maybe I can practice some of these recipes...enough to get me through." She tilted her head and bit her lip. "Could you make them simple, please? Like, really simple?"

Cheryl nodded, her face scrunched up, as though trying to remember what recipes she had planned for the show. "I don't think I did anything too hard. Although, I did have some breads in there, because it's a country theme, and of course, you have biscuits and homemade bread and rolls and..." Her voice trailed off, probably because her words had caused horror to well up hot and cold alternatively in Madeline's chest, and she was struggling to keep breathing.

"I'll take the bread out. No bread. We'll do carb-free meals. That's a way around the bread. It'll be trendy."

Madeline tried to breathe. A deep, slow breath, hold it, then let it out slow and easy, blowing, and again a slow breath. She could do this. She would not be a whinger.

Except...no. There was no way she was going to cook bread or make bread or bake bread or whatever a person did with bread. No way.

If Cheryl took the bread out and just had her, oh, pour cereal, she could do the show.

If they worked on her cooking abilities...and she practiced...maybe she would actually learn to cook in the next two weeks.

Ha. Doubtful. Since she hadn't learned in the last two years, it probably wasn't going to happen in the next two weeks. Even if she applied all of the brain cells she possessed to mastering life in the kitchen.

"Do you think you could work with me for a night or two before you leave? Maybe I can get the bread thing figured out anyway?" She managed to get those words out, although they sounded strangled, like someone had grabbed her throat. It did kind of feel like someone had a hold of her throat. Because she knew that it didn't matter how much Cheryl worked with her; she was never going to be able to bake bread or anything of the sort. They'd been trying for years to get her to be better than what she was—able to boil water and maybe dump pasta in it. Nothing more.

"You know I will. I'll cancel my flight."

"No!" Madeline held her hand up. "I will not allow you to do that. If you miss this time with your mother, I will never forgive myself. Whatever you can do before you go, that's what we'll do. And," she lifted her shoulder, forcing her lips to turn up, "if everything falls down around us, it will be embarrassing for a little bit, but it will be fine. We have enough money stashed away to live comfortably, and our cookbooks sell. We'll write more."

"We can. Are you sure?" Cheryl bit her lip, clearly more concerned Madeline was sure about Madeline than about the loss of money.

Madeline nodded her head decisively.

"Okay then. You spend the next couple of days with me, because we're going to try to bluff our way through this. If that fails, then we'll go down together."

They exchanged determined looks while Madeline put her arm around Cheryl and hugged her. "Thanks, mate."

Chapter 2

Loyal Hudson used one finger to pull the curtain back so he could peek out the picture window that faced his drive. Two newer-looking cars had just pulled in next to his house.

Almost certainly the celebrity chef and her entourage, whatever that was.

His brother Chandler had promised three camera people—and no more—a director, and the chef herself. Nothing more until the day they filmed.

The only one actually staying at his house would be the chef. The rest of them had hotel rooms in Trumbull, thirty minutes away.

The desire to run pushed through him. Since the fire and the scarring that it had left on his face, he had spent very little time in the presence of strangers.

If he kept his head tilted and angled so that only the unscarred side of his face showed, people couldn't even tell. But there was no way he was going to be able to bluff with these folks for that long.

For the first time in his life, he wished he had a housekeeper. He would go upstairs or, better yet, go out to the corral and find something to do so he wouldn't have to face this.

He didn't have to be on camera. That was a consolation. He didn't even have to be in the same room as the cameras.

He was only donating his world-class kitchen, and at this point, he even regretted doing that. Sure, he'd made a lot of money when he sold his business, and he'd rebuilt his house bigger and better after the fire, including the kitchen to cater to the one hobby he had beyond the farmwork, but if he'd known it was going to lead to this, he'd have spent the insurance money on quarter horses and lived in a tent.

THE BEAST GETS HIS COWGIRL IN THE SHOW ME STATE 15

His daughter had always loved cooking, but she loved riding horses as well.

He gritted his teeth and pulled on whatever inner reserves had enabled him to get through the pain of the skin grafts and the bandage changes and his months-long recuperation in the hospital. It was the same reserve that had allowed him to save his daughter from the fire.

It hadn't been enough to save his son.

He avoided it as much as he could, but he knew that once people saw, got over the horror, got themselves under control, his face wouldn't be an issue. He just preferred to avoid that whole uncomfortable situation.

Which probably made him a coward. Or showed a lack of character somewhere. Maybe if his wife hadn't left him at the same time, although his scars had nothing to do with the fact that she'd been cheating on him the night of the fire. She'd told him she was visiting her sick mother, and she'd have gotten away with it—like she had many times before—if it weren't for the fire and the fact that the state trooper had called her mother's and discovered she wasn't there.

Still, he couldn't get the two connected things out of his head.

Although he would hardly be interested in dating again, even if he had a whole face. Being tied to one conniving, cheating woman in his lifetime was enough. Self-torture was one character weakness he didn't have.

The people got out of their cars, and as promised, there were five of them. Three men and two women. One woman strode with confidence, shoulders thrown back, her hair cut in a no-nonsense style that did not dare to do anything but hang down in proper order at her shoulders.

Loyal didn't have a TV, so he couldn't be certain, but he was pretty sure that would be the celebrity chef. She walked with the assurance of someone who was successful. Plus, Chandler had told Loyal she was a Brit, and that woman definitely looked like the stuffy British stereotype he always thought of when he considered someone from the United Kingdom.

The other woman was much smaller, her movements quick and somehow seeming to show a sense of humor without saying a word. Her head swiveled in all directions like she'd never been in the country, let alone on a working ranch before, and her hair flew in wild disarray in every direction, even though Loyal thought it might be clipped in the back somehow.

It appeared that most of it had fallen out.

She wore jeans and a loose green blouse that rippled with the wind and hinted at a supple body underneath.

Maybe she was the director? She definitely didn't act like a celebrity as she tripped on what looked like nothing and windmilled her arms, taking two giant steps forward before she caught herself...just barely...at the edge of his porch.

One of the men laughed, a familiar laugh, friendly, and none of the others seemed surprised, like this was typical for that woman.

She turned around and said something, and they all laughed again.

Just from looking at her, he got the feeling that it would be hard to be around her and not be having a good time.

She was the kind of woman people were drawn to.

Not the kind of woman a man married.

The kind of woman who would be a great best friend.

But as she drew closer, he could see the perfect features, the angled jaw, the pointy chin, the high cheekbones, the sparkling emerald green eyes, and even the long lashes that framed those eyes in a natural, almost evocative way. Definitely at odds with the quirky way she walked and the friendly, funny impression her movements gave.

Loyal let the curtain drop back.

He wasn't interested in a beautiful woman. If he were interested in a woman at all, which he wasn't.

THE BEAST GETS HIS COWGIRL IN THE SHOW ME STATE17

Of course he was judging, but he just knew a beautiful woman would never be interested in what he had become. Not when there were scores of handsome men out there that could be hers for the taking.

People weren't supposed to judge a book by its cover. But they did.

Not that a beautiful woman couldn't have character and look beyond a man's features at the soul inside, but there really wasn't anything to see beyond his burned features anyway. His soul was black. It had been burned as well, only it hadn't had the skill of the best doctors in the country working on it. It had just withered—into smoke and ash.

The doorbell rang, and Loyal strode over, determined to keep his bland mask in place, no matter what their reactions to his face were. If he knew Chandler, and he did, being that he'd been the closest brother to him growing up, Chandler wouldn't have said a word about his face.

Or the rest of his body. Which was covered in long sleeves and jeans and boots. There was nothing to see—the scarring there was all hidden—other than the scarring on his face, and that was exactly the way it was going to stay.

The doorbell rang, and Loyal counted to three before he stepped out around the doorway, into the foyer, and opened the door.

The small, dark-haired woman stood in front with her hand out. "I'm Madeline Reese, and I hope we're at the right place. Are you Loyal?"

He wasn't expecting the British accent, and he stared.

Her head tilted to the side ever so slightly, and her eyes crinkled like she was thinking about a joke that no one else had heard. Not that she was laughing at everyone, but just that she had that inner humor along with some kind of inner light to go along with it. He'd never met anyone like her.

In his younger days, he might have said he was enraptured with her contradictions and drawn to her light.

But now, after all the things he'd been through, and looking the way he did, he would not be enraptured. He would not be interested.

He would be cool. Hard. All business.

He shook the surprise and the other odd feelings as his scarred hand came out and grasped hers, allowing his head to turn and carefully watching her face for the second she realized he wasn't perfect. That half of his face—and body—was pink and white and stretched and smooth and scarred.

Her eyes didn't widen, and the humorous look on her face didn't dim. Although her eyes did seem to search into his, like she was reading the nonverbal cues he was sending out and trying to make sense of his person. Not judging, just figuring him out.

His eyes shifted; he didn't like it. He didn't want to be figured out.

"I'm Loyal." At that second, he realized what she'd said. This was the celebrity. The chef. The millionaire. This little woman, with all her quirks and humor and brightness and, yes, that absolutely gorgeous face.

"Fantastic! The GPS stopped working about ten minutes ago, and we weren't exactly sure if we were coming to the right spot or not."

"Yeah, the mountains make the GPS kind of hard at times. Depends on which way the wind is blowing, seems like."

"But thankfully Chandler—that is your brother, correct? Chandler Hudson?"

At his nod, she continued. "Chandler gave us good directions. I think he suspected that our GPS would stop working."

"Yeah, most of them do. Every once in a while, someone has a different program that works."

He hadn't exactly thought that he would be having a run-of-the-mill, banal conversation about GPS with the celebrity chef. She kind of bemused him, reminding him a little of a butterfly that didn't sit very long in any one spot. One that, even while sitting, her wings kind of swung back and forth, opening and closing, checking the place around her, drawing in sensations, and sensing changes in the air that brushed her wings.

THE BEAST GETS HIS COWGIRL IN THE SHOW ME STATE 19

A butterfly might be an apt description, because she was beautiful like one as well.

Unsure whether he could continue to think of her as beautiful and still be unemotional about it, he pushed that thought aside to examine later.

She shifted in front of him, and he realized he was just standing there, holding his door and thinking about butterflies. Boy, if his brothers could see him now.

It was fair to say the celebrity chef had scrambled his brains. Hopefully they weren't on the menu. He had a feeling he was going to need them.

"If you don't mind, we'll come in and check out your kitchen. Are we allowed to invade?" She tilted her head and said "invade" in such a way that it almost made him smile. Before he reminded himself he was cold. He was hard. He was all business.

"I can give you a tour of the kitchen." He made his voice remain unemotional as he opened the door wider and stepped back, allowing her and the folks behind her to step into the foyer.

"Should we take our shoes off? Do you provide slippers? Maybe cowboy boots? Seems to be what everybody was wearing at the last gas station we stopped. Is it cowboy boot country?" The chef had an adorable way about her that wasn't juvenile but wasn't typical adult. Unique. It made him want to smile, and it drew him closer.

But he forced himself to focus on her question.

It was boot country. But he lifted a shoulder.

She grinned into his unemotional face like they were sharing a secret and then turned and kept bouncing along.

There was definitely no artifice in her, and it kinda threw him off. He expected someone confident and even snobby. Which was his mistake, since Chandler had been in Hollywood's world and had said that not all actors were like that. There were plenty of good actors and friendly, down-to-earth people. He didn't know why he'd been expecting something different from Madeline. But Madeline was so much more than regular, down-to-earth people.

His silence didn't seem to dim the bubbly happiness and light that glowed off her. If the camera caught that, he could understand why she was so popular. He'd barely been in her company for five minutes, but he was already hooked and knew he'd watch her do pretty much anything.

She was probably especially fun when she was doing something like cooking. Yeah, he could see how she'd become successful.

"Oh, crikey!" she exclaimed.

He blinked and closed the door, turning, startled at her cute little two-word exclamation.

"I forgot to introduce everybody. Goodness, you must think I was raised in a barn. Oh, no offense. Actually, I've never even been in a barn. Maybe I could go explore your barn, not to be pushy or anything. I don't want you to let me in your barn if I could hurt anything, although it would be kind of cool to be in a barn. Just for the fun of it. Barns seem like fun things."

She didn't seem to be uncomfortable that he didn't say anything. It was awfully hard not to smile. He couldn't remember ever fighting a smile this hard. Some people were annoying when they talked a lot, but the more she talked, the cuter she got.

Up until she walked in, he wouldn't have said someone that beautiful could be cute. But she was.

"Sorry. I got sidetracked about barns. Do you run any businesses out of your barn?" she asked, and he thought it was a serious question.

He shook his head slowly. She only needed half a second of his moving his head in a "no" before her mind was off again. "You could. There's so much character in old barns. Amazing pictures—photography would be a smart business. I've always thought restaurants would be really cool in a barn. Or a clothes shop. Wouldn't that be cool?" With that last question, she turned toward the taller woman, who looked at her with a bemused gaze as though this were a common occurrence.

"I'd never thought of it, but I could see it being fun and quirky," the woman said.

Her questions and her chatter did not seem to be from nervousness but rather from that inner light and humor.

He supposed if he were a little quicker, if he were feeling more like himself and relaxed, they would have a fun conversation.

He bet she had fun wherever she went. Even if she had to make it herself. She just seemed like that kind of woman. Not that he'd ever been around anyone like that.

The chef held her hand out. "This is Stella, the director. She'll be directing all of the shows and calling all the shots. We all listen to her." She gave a little salute like Stella was an army captain or something.

Stella smiled, and Madeline squeezed her in a one-armed hug which was returned with two arms and a cheek on the forehead.

"And these are the camera guys, they make me look good." Madeline grinned in a goofy, endearing way. "Sometimes their job is really hard. The taller one is Travis."

Travis stretched out his hand, and Loyal shook it, forgetting to look at his face to see if he noticed the scars. Madeline had taken his mind completely off them, and he'd missed anyone else's reaction.

They'd all seen by now, and they all seemed okay. Funny how Madeline could smooth things all over. Maybe her chatter was deliberate, although it seemed spontaneous and random.

"And this is Chase and Chip. They're the best camera people in Hollywood, and they certainly earn their pay making me look good." She gave them fond smiles, which were returned a hundredfold. It was obvious that the camera guys adored her, and so did Stella.

But something nagged at Loyal. In his experience, women did a lot of pretending. Her Pollyanna personality couldn't be for real. This had to be a fluke or a show she put on, no matter how authentic it seemed.

It made sense, coming from Hollywood. She was probably an actor as well as a chef.

"Okay. *Now* I think we're ready to follow you into the kitchen. Go ahead and lead the way, Mr. Hudson."

"Call me Loyal." He shouldn't have said that. Mr. Hudson was just fine for this beautiful, quirky woman who was already under his skin.

"Okay, then, Loyal. Go ahead and lead us into your kitchen. I've heard it's amazing."

He couldn't help narrowing his eyes at her just a bit as he tried to figure out what her angle was. The cheerful, almost clipped way she spoke in that accent that should make her words sound snobby but just ended up adding to the artsy and winsome atmosphere that surrounded her, so thick it was almost visual, and her relaxed acceptance of his silence and coldness definitely threw him.

Most of the time, when he froze someone out as he was doing right now, they huddled back in their shell, wounded and unwilling to allow him to continue to beat on their fragile self-esteem. Typically, people spent less than five minutes in his presence when he was full-on, hardcore ice.

Madeline didn't even seem to notice it. She met his narrowed eyes with a smile, a bright one, of her own that he would've sworn was genuine, but it couldn't be. She would not keep smiling at him when he kept not smiling back at her. It was human nature to return what you'd been given in the lowest common denominator. If one person was smiling, and one person was determined to not, the non-smiling person would win out.

Except Madeline turned that knowledge, which he would've considered an indisputable fact, completely on its ears as she continued to smile with her mouth and eyes and every muscle in between.

Her teeth were perfect, along with the arched eyebrows, and those lashes that looked like they'd been dipped in coal that contrasted with her deep green eyes. Whatever was beyond beautiful, that's what Made-

THE BEAST GETS HIS COWGIRL IN THE SHOW ME STATE 23

line was when she smiled like that. He was not going to be able to stay cold and ice if he had to continue to look into that smile.

He turned abruptly. "Follow me."

He had to fight that lightness and cheerfulness, or she would end up sucking him in. And he swore he wasn't going to fall again. Instinctively, he knew this was a woman he could fall for. Probably every man in her orbit could fall for her. Maybe she had several on the side, and from the adoring way that Travis, Chase, and Chip looked at her, they might be some of her conquests.

That's the way his ex-wife had been.

Yeah, he wasn't going down that road again.

Chapter 3

Madeline felt like her smile was going to crack her face as she followed Loyal and Stella and the camera crew into the kitchen, which was every bit as nice as she'd been told it would be. They would have no trouble filming in this: it was huge and state of the art.

She tried to be cheerful, to disarm and distract with her smile and her natural goofiness, but the man, Loyal, hadn't even allowed his lips to twitch.

If she'd ever met a more serious and seemingly sorrowful man, she couldn't recall. She supposed whatever caused the burns on his face had possibly erased the smile from it as well, so she couldn't fault him.

But she'd always had this need to have everyone love her, which was probably why it was so hard to think that she might be found out about her inability to cook.

She'd tried for the last two weeks to practice, but all she'd done was burn a lot of food and waste a lot of ingredients. Cooking took more concentration than she was used to. Not just to follow the steps but to remember to check things once they were on the stove or in the oven.

Loyal said a few short words about the kitchen, and the camera guys were discussing with Stella what the best angles were and would be with the angle of the sun and how much lighting they would need to set up.

Madeline shifted from one foot to the other. She wasn't the slightest bit interested in this either. Those guys knew their job, and her butting in wouldn't be appreciated or helpful.

Maybe Stella sensed her nervousness, because she turned to Loyal. "If you want to show Madeline where she's going be staying tonight,

THE BEAST GETS HIS COWGIRL IN THE SHOW ME STATE 25

you can go ahead. If we have any questions, we'll keep them until you get back, and then we won't hold you up."

Loyal jerked his head in acknowledgment, cut his eyes to her, jerked his head again to indicate she was to follow him, apparently, and walked from the room.

Actually, there wasn't a doorway as such. Just a shift from the kitchen to the dining room.

If Madeline were in an admiring mood, she would definitely notice how nicely the house was set up. Everything looked new too. It was none of her business to ask, although maybe if she got a chance to talk to Chandler, who she knew a little bit from being on her show over a year ago, she might be able to see if he would give her any details.

Immediately after she thought that, she shook the notion aside. It felt too much like gossip or digging for dirt, not that she was looking for dirt necessarily, but it felt intrusive. Stalkerish. Which normally she did not have a problem with, but there was something intriguing about Loyal.

Maybe it was the fact that she hadn't been able to get him to smile. She could almost always make people laugh. It bothered her. How could someone love their life if they weren't smiling?

Her eyes landed on the broad shoulders that were disappearing way in front of her. She hurried to catch up.

She had bigger things to worry about than Loyal and whether or not he was smiling.

They would film the show soon.

After that, no one was going to have any doubt in their head about her ability to cook. Or inability.

Barring a miracle.

Cheryl was in Australia, and she wasn't coming back. Her mother had just weeks to live, if that.

Loyal turned a corner and started up a wide staircase. Madeline thought she detected just a little bit of a limp, and she wondered if his burns were on more than just his face.

The back of his right hand was twisted in scars but not as badly as the skin on his face. It stood to reason that there could be more.

He didn't exactly seem like the kind of man who would welcome questions.

But she wasn't exactly the kind of woman who was put off. She nodded to herself, as though she needed the confirmation. Yes. She wasn't that kind of woman.

Following him up the stairs, admiring the rich woodwork and soaring ceilings, she said, "This looks like a new house. Did you build recently?"

"There was a fire, in case you didn't notice. And yeah, I rebuilt after the fire."

His voice was gruff and didn't welcome conversation. She almost closed her mouth and gave up. But no, she didn't give up. Ever.

"Your wife must be quite a cook. That kitchen is really something. It was nice of you to cater to her wants."

"I don't have a wife."

Oh, bother. She'd known that. Chandler had mentioned Loyal was divorced among other things. Why couldn't she engage her brain before putting her mouth in gear?

That was probably strike two. Or strike three. But they didn't have to play baseball. She could do basketball. Did one get four or five fouls before one fouled out?

"You must cook, then, and you must really love it." Or maybe he lived with his mother. Or maybe he didn't have anything to do with designing the house that he built. It felt like she was banging her head against a wall.

Even more so as the seconds ticked by, they reached the top of the stairs, and he never answered her.

THE BEAST GETS HIS COWGIRL IN THE SHOW ME STATE 27

All right. So she had a small issue where she wanted everyone to love her and be her friend. Not something people expected from a Brit, she could admit. But it was the way she was. So she couldn't give up.

He began walking down the hall, and she continued to follow him, gathering her internal reserves, taking a breath, and asking another question.

"Did you get your scars in the fire that burned the house down?" Oh well. Yes. Madeline was definitely forcing it a bit too much. Couldn't she have broached an obviously less sensitive topic?

He stopped abruptly. She was so busy castigating herself she almost ran into his back. When he turned around, they were practically nose to nose. Or nose to forehead, which would be taking into account their height differences. She did not love being short.

"Yes. My scars are from the house fire. Would you like to see them all?" he asked in a fake-gracious tone. "I have them the entire way along my right side. From the burning beam that fell on me as I was trying to rescue my son." He held his hands up like he would start to take off his shirt.

Once, when she'd been younger, she and a friend back in England had climbed over the fence in their garden and jumped into their neighbors' garden where they'd been sunbathing. Nude.

She felt a little bit now like she did back then, like she wished she'd stayed on her own side of the fence. Like as soon as she saw the naked bodies of her neighbors, she'd wished she'd never climbed it and wished she was back in her own garden on her own side.

Fences were there for a reason. Definitely the wall Loyal had put up between them was there for a reason. He wasn't very happy that she had bull-dozed her way through it.

"I'm sorry," she said to his chin. "I definitely have a tendency to say things I shouldn't, and I have even more of a tendency to..." There was a big pause here while she tried to figure out how she could say what her flaw was without actually saying it. But then she decided that he'd just been very blunt with her about his scars and the fire and the fact that he had lost a son, so she decided she could be blunt too. "I can't stand it when people don't like me, and I guess I do keep working until I get them to act like they do or until they hate me. Obviously, you belong to the latter category, and I apologize."

She thought he'd probably let it go at that, as austere and taciturn as he had been.

But as her eyes stayed glued to his chin, it started moving.

"I guess you remind me of my ex-wife. She wanted everyone to like her too. And by 'like,' I mean in a physical sense."

He kind of let the words hang there, and she probably should have been pondering them, since they seemed very serious, but she'd actually been watching his chin move up and down, and it was a rather nice chin. With short stubble on it and a little cleft. The scars on the right side of his face stopped an inch or two short from his chin, leaving it whole and perfect. It was definitely perfect.

"You're looking at me like you have no idea what I was talking about. Tell me you know what I mean by 'physical sense.'"

There seemed to be a softening of his jaw, not quite a smile, or maybe it was her imagination.

She gave a mental blink and tried to pull her mind back from the rabbit trail it was on this time. There always seemed to be a lot of rabbit trails up there for it to hop down.

"I do. That's definitely not me. I'm not really a touchy-feely person." Not with people she didn't know.

"I guess we all have our little hang-ups." Could that be a touch of humor in his voice?

But as her eyes skimmed across his face, she didn't see any uptick of his lip or even a twinkle in his eyes.

"I agree," she said, giving up looking for a smile. "We all have our things."

"Some of us have more than others," he said abruptly before whirling and continuing down the hall.

She walked after him, a little slower. Bemused at the swirl in her chest and the odd way her fingers itched, almost like she actually did want to reach out and skim them over his skin. Definitely odd, since she'd never been tempted to do anything like that before.

She hadn't been lying to him about her aversion to touching strangers.

That desire to touch was definitely new. She wasn't quite sure whether she liked it.

No. She knew for a fact she did *not* like it. Especially not with that man. Why couldn't she have that desire for some nice, genial, pleasant guy?

He opened the door at the far end of the hall, and she lengthened her stride so she wasn't too far behind him.

"This is your room."

He stepped back. She stepped in.

Everything was white. The bedspread, the walls, the carpet, the dresser, the curtains…even the clock was a white color.

"It's very white." Maybe she was stating the obvious, but she couldn't think of anything else to say. Other than, "It will do perfectly, thank you."

"My room is out at the other end of the hall, so you have this side of the house to yourself." He was already backing out of the room and turning to leave. "Can you find your way back down?"

"I'm coming. There's no need for me to stay. I'll have to get my stuff and carry it up later."

"I'll carry it up. It's still in the car?"

"Yes," she said, appreciative that he had offered.

She followed him, inhaling deeply, enjoying and cataloging the scent that she now recognized as his. Something low and subtle, reminding her of dark nights and sultry voices and maybe the twang of a guitar combined with starlight and moonlight and his subtle freshness that she couldn't quite put her finger on but couldn't stop breathing in. It made her heart flutter, and her hands itched to touch again.

She'd wanted to be friends with Loyal and had looked forward to getting to know him, even if it was only for a couple of days until her secret was exposed.

But now, after this odd reaction, she thought that maybe the best thing for her to do would be to stay completely away from him.

Chapter 4

When they got to the kitchen, Stella was on the phone. It was obvious from her agitated position, the way she paced back and forth, and the short bursts of words that came out of her mouth periodically that something was going on.

Madeline had only been in the business for two years, but she would say something big. Really big.

And from the way Stella's eyes widened and her posture changed when Madeline walked in, she would definitely say this big thing was most certainly about her.

Normally, this would thrill her beyond words. She loved the excitement of the business and the way it worked and jumping on opportunities and turning them into profitable activities. But excitement mixed with dread in her stomach, creating a twisted, sour feeling that made her want to keep walking right out of the kitchen.

She hadn't gotten where she was by walking away from new opportunities.

The only difference now was Cheryl had always been by her side. She couldn't have quite the same excitement and eagerness for a new opportunity when Cheryl couldn't be there to back her up since they'd always stepped into every new thing together.

"Let me talk to her, and I'll call you right back." Stella swiped off her phone and turned immediately to Madeline, her hands clasped together in front of her and her eyes practically glowing. "I would ask to go outside and talk to you, but I think everyone here is going to need to hear this eventually, although you do have the final say. You'll probably want to talk it over with Cheryl, since you two make decisions together, even though she's not here."

Her excitement was contagious, and it had begun to take over all of the dread that had been sticking and hardening in Madeline's chest. Whatever it was, it was going to be amazing, and she could handle it. She *would* handle it. Cooking, she was no good at. But business opportunities, she was all over them. She would figure this out.

But first, she needed to know what it was.

Crossing her arms over her chest, she did her best to concentrate.

Out of the corner of her eye, she could see Loyal's hands crossed over his chest and his feet planted while he waited. Hopefully whatever Stella had in mind was something he would go along with.

"Ricardo Novello, the network's biggest live show sensation, is down with pneumonia. His doctor said at least six, maybe eight, weeks out." Stella tried to look sad about Ricardo being ill, but then she ruined the effort because she lowered her voice, leaned forward, and said with barely suppressed excitement, "The network executives want *you* to take his place." She let out a little squeal and a hop. Surprising, since Madeline had never seen much of anything except cool reserve and occasional light affection from Stella before.

Madeline felt like hopping and squealing almost as much as she felt like screaming and running and pulling her hair out.

Why now? Now, when Cheryl wasn't here, they'd been offered the biggest break that they'd had so far in their career, and she would have to let it go. There was no way, *no way*, she could do a live show.

"The first live show is next week. I told him we'd be ready. It is going to change the schedule some though," she said, looking over at Loyal, a touch of uncertainty crimping her face. "I know we're already imposing and playing on your loyalty to your brother, Chandler, but this means that we would need at least six weeks here, because we could only do one show per week and would have to be live."

Stella tapped her clipboard. "Of course, there are also the considerations that there couldn't be any people coming in and out during the time we're filming and some other things that we would need to hash out. So, total change of plans. But they're willing to pay big bucks because we sent them some photos of the kitchen, and it's perfect. We can blend the country kitchen with 'live,' and everyone will love it!" She ended her speech with a hopeful look at Loyal, and her head tilted and nodded, as though encouraging him to just say yes.

The look on his face wasn't encouraging.

Should Madeline be happy about that—that he seemed like he was going to say no—or should she jump up and try talking him into it?

A war raged in her own chest. How much longer would Cheryl be in Australia? Madeline checked the time, realizing Cheryl would be in bed right now. She would call her before she went to bed tonight. Maybe if she could bluff her way through the first show, Cheryl would be back in time to do the rest.

"I don't..."

"Loyal," Madeline interrupted him before he could decline. "Would you walk outside with me for second so we can chat for just a moment?" She was taking a risk by asking him for what amounted to a favor. He had no reason to give it to her. They weren't friends or even business associates. He had only just met her and didn't even seem to like her.

Before he answered her, he pulled his phone out of his pocket and looked down, maybe reading a text since his eyes went back and forth several times.

The text apparently wasn't good news, because he wasn't smiling. If anything, his face pinched tighter than it had been when he was going to say no.

"I really don't have a lot of time." He finally looked up.

"This won't take long."

Loyal flattened his lips and didn't look any more eager to walk outside with her than he had two minutes ago, but he jerked his chin, and she went out the closest door, which led to a covered brick patio.

She waited for the door to close behind him. She hadn't wanted to play this card and had hoped that she wouldn't have to, but she had spoken to Chandler for a few minutes on the phone when they were setting this up. Chandler had said that Loyal probably wouldn't be very interested, but he gave her a few insider tips that she might be able to use as bargaining chips. It wasn't the way she wanted to do business, but sometimes she had to pull out all the stops in order to make things work.

This felt like one of those times.

"I don't want to take up too much of your time, so I'll just play straight with you. When I spoke with Chandler, he mentioned that you had a daughter who didn't want to stay with you, because you scared her." She hated to say that, and he winced like she'd hit him, which she really probably had. Not a physical blow, but one of those heart blows that hurt worse, the ones where you'd rather have been punched in the stomach, because physical pain faded a lot faster.

"I'm not talking about that with you."

His words were finite, like the subject was closed, and they succeeded in hitting her back. She didn't flinch.

Maybe the subject really was closed, but she wanted to help him, not hurt him. It was true she was looking for a means to the end for her, but not if it involved making him suffer. This should, hopefully, involve helping him get what he wanted.

"I have always been pretty good with kids. When Chandler was on the set with me, we had a preschool group in, which is what I think made him think of me in this position. Because for some reason, kids just love me." It was totally true. And she had no idea why. Other than possibly the experience she had with her triplet sisters who were twelve years younger than she was. She'd spent plenty of time with little children.

"I'm almost positive that your daughter and I will get along, enough that your ex will let her stay. Chandler said that she has full custody, that she will walk away if your daughter cries, and she won't take enough time to stay so that you can get your daughter to become comfortable with you."

There. She kind of spit it all out. Normally she was a better negotiator, but the closed-off look on his face and the folded arms combined with the scent that pulled her from inside and that odd feeling of wanting to touch him put her a little off-kilter.

Children she could snuggle with, she'd never had a problem. Adults, not so much.

Except, apparently, Loyal.

Breaking one of her own rules of negotiation, she turned her back on the person she was negotiating with and looked out across the rolling hills of Missouri. Brown now, and chilly. Typical, probably, for January.

If he didn't agree, they'd just have to find a different kitchen; that was all. Or something.

But for some reason, she wanted to be here with Loyal.

Which was probably a good enough reason to go.

But she'd never been a quitter either, and now that she had her heart set on this, she really wanted it to happen. The idea of a man like Loyal not being able to spend time with his daughter because she cried when she saw him tore at her heartstrings.

It also made her want to grab his ex-wife by her hair because that had to be a sucker punch to his heart every time.

She whirled back around. "Do you want to have a relationship with your daughter? I can help you with that. All you have to do is open up your kitchen and your house for the next six weeks." She shook her head and looked off in the distance.

No. She didn't want to include that in the bargaining. She couldn't. The more she thought about it… "Never mind," she said abruptly. "Forget everything I just said. This isn't contingent on you hosting the cooking show. I'm just making an offer. If you want me to try to help you with your daughter, you don't have to give me anything in return. I'll just do it."

His eyes had narrowed, and he seemed to glare at her. "My mother and my sister-in-law both have helped me, and she won't quit crying for either one of them. I hardly think a complete stranger and nonfamily member will have any better success."

"Are you willing to try?"

"Now that I'm completely healed, I'm going to fight for custody. I'm going to at least get the time that should be rightfully mine with her. When she gets to know me again, she won't cry anymore." He hadn't answered her question, almost like he was telling himself things that he hadn't quite figured out.

"How long is that going to take? And are you guaranteed a judge is actually going to award you custody? Isn't that pretty unusual for the dad to get?"

His lips flattened, and he turned away. Obviously, he'd already thought of that. Most of the time, if the mother was doing a good job, it was an uphill battle for the father to be included in a fair way. Things were changing, but it depended a lot on the judge.

He pursed his lips, and his shoulders seemed to slump a little. He knew she was right. "My ex isn't unreasonable. I wouldn't even need to go to a judge, and we could work things out between us, but she claims that our daughter has already been through enough, and she can't allow her to stay when she's crying uncontrollably." He squared his jaw, kind of narrowed his eyes, and looked at her with an assessing look. "She was burned, too, in the fire. In that, my ex is right. She's been through enough."

The look he gave her, calculating, like he wasn't sure whether she could handle things, made her wonder exactly how bad the little girl had been burned.

It didn't matter for her purposes now, though. "It's not like I'm going to like a little girl less because she has burn scars." She paused. "That applies to everyone, for that matter." Her meaning was not subtle, and she was sure it was not lost on him.

He ignored any implications about himself. "I didn't think you would. I just felt like I needed to say it."

"It's been said. Unnecessarily."

"So if I agree to the six weeks, are you staying here for the six weeks solid? Are you going back and forth between here and Hollywood?"

"I don't fly. Much." She left it at that. "That would be a lot of driving to do every week, but if you don't want me here, I can try to find somewhere else to stay."

"You're afraid of flying?"

She tossed her head and wiggled her brows. "I can do it. It just takes a lot of pills."

She thought his lips might have twitched at that. She purposely said it flippantly, but it was the absolute truth. She'd flown across the ocean. But there was just something about being trapped in the airplane that brought her claustrophobia to the surface and gave her panic attacks.

He looked over at the cars sitting in the driveway. "I guess they do have California license plates on them."

"Yes. They cater to me. I'm sure though, if we go through with this live thing, they'll fly back and forth. It sounds like it's going to be lucrative enough for the studio to foot the bill." She turned back to him. "Your kitchen is amazing. I've never seen a kitchen like that in a personal home, not that I've been in a lot of them, but it's the kind of kitchen that you might find in a mansion somewhere, not on a farm in Missouri."

His arms had uncrossed, and he shoved his hands in his pockets. His stance was still not welcoming, but he seemed to at least have taken down a few bricks of the wall that he'd built between them. "The fire that killed my son started in the kitchen. I will not allow that to happen again."

With that statement, everything made sense, and things clicked in her mind.

Of course.

The fire might have even been because of something he'd done. Chandler had said that cooking was a big hobby of Loyal's.

Maybe he'd left the stove on, or maybe he'd been cooking the night of the fire. She couldn't probe any more, but it didn't take a psychiatrist to see that he blamed himself for his son's death, and that the state-of-the-art kitchen was less about catering to his hobby and more about penance or defense. Meaning, like he said, it was never going to happen again.

He let out a breath and pulled his hands out of his pockets. "If you give me a hand with Patty, and even if you won't, the kitchen is yours for as long as you want it. Just let me know what I need to do."

Just like that? She tried to keep the shocked look off her face, wondering what had changed his mind. "I'm sure they're going to compensate you for it," she said as he was turning.

"Money doesn't matter. I just appreciate your offer, that you were willing to help me, even if I said no. I wasn't expecting that." His jaw jutted out as he looked at the floor. "People don't often surprise me quite that much."

She certainly hadn't been expecting him to admit it. But she wasn't going to go there. "How far away does your ex live? When will be the next time she'll bring Patty? And maybe sometime we could talk about what Patty likes, and you can give me an idea of the best ways to connect with her and things that I can do."

"She's actually scheduled to visit her parents this weekend. Let me think for a few hours. I've got work to do out here."

"Okay," she said, falling in line behind him as he put his hand on the doorknob.

He stopped and looked over his shoulder. "One more thing. When you guys are filming, I will not be in the house. At all. That's my one stipulation."

She nodded, even though contract negotiations weren't her area. "Fair enough."

She could understand why he wouldn't want to be anywhere near a camera. Not that she thought he was ugly, but she could understand not wanting to be reminded. From experience, she knew the camera could be unforgiving, and every flaw was magnified. "I'll make sure that that's in the contract."

When he looked at her, she almost thought, for the first time since she'd met him, there was a little bit of warmth in his eyes as he looked down at her.

She also had a feeling that this was one of those turns in the road that would change her life in ways too many to go back from.

Hopefully all good.

Maybe she was imagining it all, but she smiled big anyway. "Thanks a lot. I appreciate this, Loyal."

Chapter 5

Loyal stood in his bedroom window, staring out at the winter fields, all resting. Cold wind blew over them tonight, and he was grateful for the warmth inside.

He'd signed a pretty big contract today, and he hadn't been able to sleep.

It wasn't the money that had him upset though.

Madeline.

She had not been what he expected, from the first. He hadn't expected her offer today, either.

Part of him wished he'd tested her on it. Not given in so easily. Just to see if she really would have done what she said she would—work with him on getting his daughter to accept him without any payment in return. But part of him didn't want to expose that weakness to her—that his own daughter couldn't even stand to look at him.

Madeline had sounded serious, and she'd said that she didn't require anything in return. He could've turned down her network's contract and withdrawn the offer of using his "country kitchen."

The kind of generosity she had shown had taken him unaware.

After he thought about it for a second, he couldn't let her offer go without making one of his own.

Isn't that what tended to happen when people were kind? Kindness bred kindness?

Maybe not in everyone, but it sure inspired it in him.

Still, he didn't exactly have buyer's remorse, but he did wonder what in the world he'd gotten into.

She was like his ex-wife all over again.

That comparison was unfair, and he knew it. His brain was insisting on it because his heart couldn't take another split like the one he'd already survived. Barely.

Madeline was friendlier—quirkier, definitely—and a little more...real, maybe. But she was the kind of woman that drew men like flies.

He could feel the pull she exerted on him, and he fought it. Not only because there was no hope for them, but because he wasn't going to fall for another woman who was not content with just one man.

He wasn't sleepy, but he'd just decided to go back to bed when he heard the click of a door and a soft voice out in the hall.

He shouldn't be concerned about her. She could do whatever she wanted to, including slip out in the middle of the night, but hey, he could also do whatever he wanted to do, and if he wanted to go downstairs and get a drink of water at the sink, he sure could.

Just because he hadn't wanted to do it three seconds ago—before he'd heard the voice—didn't mean anything.

If he were being honest with himself, he had to admit there was some kind of attraction there, for him, anyway, toward Madeline, but he knew he had to protect himself from it.

He'd already been burned once badly; he wasn't going to allow it to happen again. If he could just see that she was sneaking around in the middle of the night, it would be all his heart needed to realize that no matter what the attraction was, she was completely off-limits, because he wasn't going through that again.

Opening his door quietly, he slipped out into the dark hall. Almost immediately, her voice came more clearly, and he could just see her white T-shirt disappearing down the steps.

Eavesdropping was rude, but it wasn't wrong. There was no verse in the Bible that forbid it, at least not one that he learned in Sunday School or ever sat under a preaching about.

So, with only a small twinge of guilt, he stood against the wall, listening to Madeline's voice.

"Yes. It's live."

The person she was talking to must've been on speaker, because he could hear her voice crackling through the phone. "How are you going to do that? What are you going to do? You need to find someone."

"I know." Madeline's voice sounded resigned.

Loyal walked softly to the steps.

She disappeared through the dining room and into the kitchen, so he slipped down, still listening.

"I thought about hiring someone. But, I mean, who? It has to be someone trustworthy, who can keep our secret. Otherwise, the point is moot. But it also has to be someone who's good. Really good. Someone that I can count on to have our best interests at heart."

"That's for sure. There is no point hiring someone who's just going to out us to the rest of the world. You might as well do that yourself. Because it's gonna look a hundred times worse if you try to cover it up."

Grim satisfaction, underlined by a quiet ill ease, settled in Loyal's chest. He'd known it.

Madeline had a secret. Something pretty bad by the sounds of things. He had been right not to trust her.

Okay. So he hadn't exactly had any thoughts about not trusting her, but he should have. Obviously, she was not trustworthy. What could she be hiding?

He'd reached the bottom of the steps and slipped closer, straining to hear every word.

"Yes. That's exactly what I thought. So, that's why I was calling you. But if your mom's not doing well..."

"No. I can hire someone to take care of her, and she probably will end up in hospice, but not tomorrow. These are definitely her last days. I can come back, but I know I'll always regret it."

THE BEAST GETS HIS COWGIRL IN THE SHOW ME STATE

Obviously, whoever that was, her mother was dying. Loyal's heart twisted. His mom would help him. She'd do what Madeline had offered to do, if she could. But he could see where Madeline might be able to succeed where his mother had failed. She just had that way about her—sweet and funny and endearing—that attracted people. Kids would surely see it too.

"No. I won't let you. You stay there. You can never get this time back. We agreed before you left that we were both okay if this whole thing blew up, because your mother is more important. I still feel that way. I'm sure you do too."

"Yes. But I do feel torn, because I know you need me."

"I need you, but I can find someone else. I just need a little bit of time. Which I'm running out of. If only I weren't so deathly afraid of airplanes. I need someone to fly with me so I can take enough pills to make the flight."

The person on the other end of the phone laughed, a tinkling, sweet sound. "It's always fun to fly with you, those pills really relax you, and I never have any idea what's coming out of your mouth. I could make a lot of money with the videos I take."

"Keep them," Madeline said easily. "You can blackmail me someday." Her voice held humor and unlimited trust, like she knew the person on the other end of the line would never betray her like that.

A sister?

That's the way Loyal felt about his brothers and maybe a few men in his town. There weren't too many people who got unlimited trust like that.

"I fully intend to." The person on the other line made a thoughtful sound. "Maybe that's what I can do if this whole thing blows up. I'll dig those old airplane videos out and see if I can't get any of the gossip rags to bite on them."

"I don't think there are gossip rags anymore. They're like websites now. I hope you find one."

"Hey, thank you, my friend."

"It's the least I can do, for being incapable of learning how to cook."

"It's not your fault."

"I still feel guilty."

The voices kind of faded off as Loyal stood there with his mouth open. He was pretty sure that the world-famous chef Madeline Reese had just admitted that she *wasn't able to cook*.

That was a pretty big bombshell. And he didn't even know her, didn't watch TV. For her fans, that would be huge. No wonder she was wandering around in the middle of the night whispering into her phone.

No wonder she was worried about her performance of a lifetime.

What in the world was she planning on doing? What did she mean by hiring someone? Who was this person she was talking to? Did that person somehow help her cook?

He supposed technology was advanced to the point that she could have some kind of earpiece in that would enable a person to tell her what to do while that person was watching in person or on a monitor. It wasn't hard for him to hazard a few guesses in that direction. Pretty accurate guesses, probably. It could hardly be anything else, since she'd said with her own mouth she was *unable to cook*.

How had she managed to create a cooking empire without being able to cook?

He'd heard enough. He knew exactly what the midnight conversation was about, and he slipped away, stepping quietly up the stairs and going back to his room. Still not any more sleepy than he had been when he left but feeling a good bit wiser.

It really wasn't his concern, or any of his business, unless Madeline wasn't the kind of person to keep her word, because if her show failed and she left, he wouldn't have anyone to help him with Patty and Lisa.

He checked his watch. Midnight. It would only be ten o'clock on the Oregon coast where they lived. Her monthly visit with her moth-

THE BEAST GETS HIS COWGIRL IN THE SHOW ME STATE

er was this coming week. Before Madeline, he'd been going to let it go and deal with this through their lawyers, but with Madeline's offer—he still couldn't get over that she had said she'd do it without him doing anything in return and wished he'd tested her on that—he thought for a few minutes on how to word it correctly before he sent off a text.

Originally Loyal had thought it was horrible timing that the Hollywood people wanted to come at the same time that his wife was flying in to visit her parents.

She always said she would drop Patty off, and she claimed that he could have his fair time with her too, but she'd never actually done it, because if Lisa left the room, Patty wouldn't stop screaming as long as he was there.

Patty definitely wouldn't stand to be alone with him. It had been that way since the fire.

Sometimes he wondered if she associated him with her nightmarish memories. Of course, he had been there—and Lisa had not—but he'd been saving Patty's life.

Still, she might associate him with the pain of her burns. Plus, his looks had been forever altered, and not in a good way.

But for now, he was kind of excited about the fact that Madeline would be here. Maybe she had the personality to get through to Patty, and he could possibly spend time with his daughter *this week*.

Then reality took over, and he realized that she probably wasn't going to be able to work a miracle that no one else had been able to work. His mother had tried; even his ex, Lisa, had said she'd tried to get Patty to not be petrified of him.

But if Madeline could get Patty to not cry, then he would probably be able to get Lisa to let Patty stay with him for a bit. Maybe even longer than her normal weeklong visit with her parents.

Schooling wouldn't be a problem, since Lisa had Patty doing online school anyway.

Most of him said it wouldn't work out, but there was a part of him that couldn't help but be hopeful.

Chapter 6

"Not the cucumbers, the green peppers. You needed the bowl of green peppers."

Madeline's head pounded, and the spot directly between her shoulder blades ached like there was a sword stuck there. Her feet hurt, and she was pretty sure sweat was trickling down her temple. But she was cooking, and she wasn't going to wipe her forehead, as much as she wanted to. She had grabbed the bowl of green things, which weren't really green...why couldn't she remember what cucumbers looked like?

Sometimes, Cheryl and she would even number the bowls, so all Cheryl had to do was call a number in her ear.

Stella had no idea. Although Stella was completely vested in her success, she had a lot of other clients who were competitive. They'd never felt like they could trust her completely because it just might be easier—and more lucrative—for her to let the cat out of the bag, so to speak, sell them out to a gossip site, and have one of her other clients take their spot at the top. Many of them were just as talented—using that word loosely—as Madeline, although they didn't have her quirky humor.

Of course, no one knew her quirky humor was a direct result of her complete inability to cook anything.

She lifted the bowl of cucumbers and dumped them into the frying pan.

"No! No! That's not where they go. You were supposed to..." Stella yanked her headset off her head and looked up at the ceiling. "I understand your concern about Cheryl and her mother and that you miss her. But your head is just not in this today. You have got to do better! This was supposed to be just an easy-peasy run-through, setting up camera angles and trying out Cheryl's latest recipe. It was not supposed to be a comedy of errors... It's not even a comedy. It's a flipping tragedy!" She threw her hands in the air. "I think we all need to take ten." She didn't say anything else before stomping out of the kitchen, through the living room, and out the front door, slamming it behind her.

Chip, Travis, and Chase followed her with their eyes, then all three of them looked back at Madeline. She wanted to think that they were friendly and on her side, but she knew better. They might not say anything, because working on her show was a privilege and was one of the better-paying gigs, even if it did require travel once in a while, like now, but they were irritated. This wasn't supposed to turn into an hours-long thing. It was supposed to be short and done quickly so they could go do whatever they wanted to for the rest of the day.

"I'm sorry, guys." That's all she could say. It was only going to get worse from here. She could, and probably would, spend the rest of the day studying this stupid recipe and still not know what was supposed to go on when and how.

"Maybe you wanna turn those cucumbers off. They're burning. And you don't cook cucumbers anyway." Travis ran a hand over his head, pulling off his headset in one smooth motion and hooking it on the side of his camera stand. "I'm gonna take a smoke break. I'll be outside if you need me."

The other guys followed suit, and all three traipsed out.

Madeline looked around her at the ingredients still sitting out to use and the ones she'd messed up. The bowls and pans and utensils. Everything she needed to do her job.

Feeling more like crying than she had in a really long time, she put her arms on the counter, pushing the bowls out of the way, and put her head down on top of them, her eyes close up to the countertop.

What was she going to do?

THE BEAST GETS HIS COWGIRL IN THE SHOW ME STATE

Maybe she should just tell everyone now and get it all over with. They might be able to find another substitution for the show next week.

After they finished here today, they had the afternoon off and the entire weekend. That would be enough time. Probably.

From what she understood, Loyal's daughter was coming tomorrow afternoon.

She'd promised to help him with her, but if she told everyone her secret today, they'd be packing up and going back to Hollywood.

She'd be fired.

She could probably stay as long as she wanted if she was able to help with Patty, though Loyal might not want someone who lived such a huge lie in front of an entire country helping with his daughter.

Because of her little sisters, the triplets, and her ability with children, she was pretty sure she could give him a hand and at least get his daughter to not cry and hopefully get his ex to let her stay.

If he'd overlook her lack of character.

Straightening, she went to turn and grab the recipe to study it some more, not that that would help her tell the difference between green peppers and cucumbers. Especially when they were both chopped up the same. One of them was brighter green. Peppers?

As she shifted, she thought she saw a shadow moving through the living room near the hall. But when her eyes refocused on the spot, whatever it was was gone. If it was anything at all. It might just be a reflection from the tears that had pooled in her eyes but she hadn't allowed to fall.

Maybe she could call Cheryl and see if Cheryl could simplify this recipe even more. It was supposed to be some kind of cucumber salsa with some type of beef roast.

The dinner rolls that Cheryl had originally included had been axed. Madeline was pretty sure she could handle the roast. If she could just figure out which bowl held peppers and which bowl contained cucumbers.

It wasn't like she could ask anyone.

The onions she got. She might have to smell them, but once she figured it out, she could write onions on the container.

She squared her shoulders; she could bloody well pull this off. Somehow.

The rest of the practice didn't go any better, and that night found Madeline up again.

She didn't bother calling Cheryl. She couldn't help her, and she was busy with her mum. Madeline had sent her a couple of quick texts checking on her, and her mum was about the same. Madeline didn't want to call and bother her over something that Cheryl wouldn't be able to fix. It would only make her feel guilty for not being here.

The moon was pretty close to being full, and the yellow glow came in the southern-facing windows, giving the furniture gray forms as she wandered through the living room, into the dining room, and finally to the kitchen.

She didn't need to turn the lights on but pulled a stool out and sat down at the bar, putting both elbows on the countertop and setting her cheeks down on her hands.

The rest of the practice after Stella and the camera crew had come back had been an unmitigated disaster. She'd thought green peppers and cucumbers were hard to tell apart, but when they added zucchini to the mix, she was completely lost. It was awful.

Stella had lost the plot once more, huffing out, and Madeline considered it a small miracle that the woman still had hair.

The camera crew were upset with her to say the very least, and she kind of thought they figured she was doing it on purpose—part of her quirky personality.

If only.

THE BEAST GETS HIS COWGIRL IN THE SHOW ME STATE

She'd definitely dropped a clanger, and most certainly not on purpose.

The only reason that Stella hadn't completely given up was probably that they all thought she was goofing—although, in her defense, she'd never "goofed" like this. If they all knew that she wasn't goofing off at all, that she really was this incompetent in the kitchen, they'd be bailing.

There was no hope for the show.

Her conscience dictated that she needed to tell everyone before next week.

Consideration demanded she tell them now while there was still hope to find a replacement.

But the cowardly part of her was strong, and she didn't want to face the music. Or maybe it was the greedy part of her that didn't want to give up the lucrative career that she'd spent two years building with Cheryl.

She'd certainly never tried to pretend it was anything but Cheryl and her as a team. She might be the face, but Cheryl had always been behind her. Neither one of them would have been successful without the other. Madeline had no problem admitting that. She wasn't trying to take anything from Cheryl. In fact, if anything, she was trying to hold it together for Cheryl.

Because not only was Cheryl dealing with her mom, but she was also dealing with the potential collapse of their very successful and satisfying business. Madeline hated that she was adding to her stress load.

But there was nothing she could do about it.

She sighed, feeling like her breath was coming out from the very bottoms of her toes.

One other issue holding her back was her irritating desire that bordered on need to have everyone like her. There were going to be a lot of haters when this came out. No one looked forward to being hated, she was sure, but she was such a people pleaser it was especially hard.

Probably at first it would be difficult for anyone to believe she was as incompetent in the kitchen as she was. Not after all the cooking shows she'd done, all the vegetables she'd worked with, all the food she'd prepared...surely some of it had sunk in. But just like some people had a learning block with mathematics, some people were tone-deaf, and some people couldn't match clothes and colors, she was completely incompetent in the kitchen.

Always had been, probably always would be.

She didn't know what to do about it.

"We both seem to be nocturnal wanderers."

The voice startled her, and she jerked up and back, upsetting the stool and sending it crashing to the floor. Luckily, she was able to stay on her feet.

After the crash, the kitchen was eerily silent.

A form shifted out of the shadows. "Sorry. I guess that means I scared you."

"I guess it does." She couldn't keep a little irritation out of her voice, but there was a lot of relief there too. There wasn't anything scary about the house, and nothing even the slightest bit odd had happened to her. Her reaction was more a sign of the internal anxiety and debate from not knowing what to do about the show. "I guess I just wasn't expecting another voice. I was listening to the ones in my head."

"What are they saying?" Loyal's shadowy figure walked around and sat down across from her at the bar.

"They're saying that I'm a fool." She didn't think he'd seen the practice session today. The contract said that he would be outside while they were filming and didn't have to be anywhere near them. She assumed it was because he didn't want to be around the cameras, although he hadn't come right out and said that. But he'd made it clear he didn't want to have anything to do with the show, so he'd probably been far away and had no clue what was going on or how close she was to losing everything.

"Why are they saying that?" His voice was surprisingly gentle.

After her interactions with him, she didn't think of him as a gentle man. But it was dark enough that she couldn't see his features, could barely make out the outline of his hands against the light bar top, and she didn't expend much energy trying to reconcile the picture she had in her mind with the voice that was coming from him tonight.

"I don't know," she muttered. "I guess because I couldn't do anything right today." To say the least.

Maybe it was a sign of how desperate she was, but she had to remind herself that this man was one of the people she had to fool. He certainly wasn't a confidant, no matter how gentle his voice sounded. No matter how different he was tonight from the man she had talked to when she first came. The one she had made a deal with.

Which reminded her. "Our deal is still on if that's what you're concerned about. Just because I'm up in the middle of the night doesn't mean I'm not going to help you tomorrow when your daughter arrives."

"I wasn't worried about that. When you offered to help me and didn't make it contingent on me doing something for you, I kinda figured you were a better person than what I'd originally judged you to be." He shifted. Maybe it was a shoulder lifting. She wasn't sure. "I have to admit I didn't judge very well to begin with."

"That's funny, because I have a tendency to give people more than the benefit of the doubt, to assume that they're far better than what they actually are, and only immediate evidence, in my face, will change my mind."

"Yeah. That makes us different all right. I've found that low expectations cause less pain."

She found that sad. "That's partly true. I guess I've just never lived my life based on the amount of pain that I think I'm going to incur. Maybe your way is a smarter way to live."

"No. It's not. It's a defense mechanism. After you've already been hurt so much, you start to feel like you can't take any more."

Maybe he was talking about his ex-wife cheating on him—rumors she'd heard, nothing based on fact. Assuming it was true, she didn't know how long they'd been married before he found out. Or even if they'd stayed married after he knew about it. Some people did. Just for the children, or the fact that they were in business together or in politics together, or some other reason that might keep them thinking that their partnership was important even if they weren't monogamous.

She couldn't imagine staying in a relationship like that. But she didn't imagine herself in many relationships anyway. She hadn't finished establishing her career, and she didn't want to lose her focus. A boyfriend would definitely take her focus away from becoming the top chef in the world.

Ironic, since she couldn't cook. That irony was not lost on her.

Her current problem.

"You didn't have anything to say to that. Haven't you ever been hurt?"

She suspected, if it weren't completely dark, he would never have asked that question. It didn't sound like a question that felt natural to a man like him. But as she thought of the scars on his face and how the darkness hid them, it probably emboldened him, and maybe things that he'd like to say during the day slipped out in the dark.

"I've been hurt, certainly. But I've never had a spouse cheat on me, if that's what you're asking. That would be hard since I've never been married. But I suppose the more successful a person is, the more people there are who are shooting at you. That hurts."

There was time before he spoke again for him to take four or five good, slow breaths.

His voice was a little hesitant. "When you're not successful, there's nothing for people to shoot at. It's when you start to rise that people start to see you as a target, and if or when they can't make themselves better on their own, they try to shoot you down." He laughed without humor. "That's pretty common. I suppose it would be almost expected in Hollywood. No worse place for that type of thing."

"I'm sure you're right. Fake friends, because everyone wants to be your friend, but those same friends are causally using you, trying to get ahead of you, no matter what it takes." She'd never thought about it and hadn't realized that there had been a lot of hurt until she heard the bitterness in her voice.

She brushed it off. There had been people that she'd helped that had turned around and stabbed her in the back. People that she'd had on her show, or people that had done her show as a guest host, then had gone out and said unkind things and downright untrue things.

He spoke while she was still considering. "Surely success makes up for that, though. I mean, you're making enough money that it shouldn't matter what other people say about you."

A common misconception. "That makes sense. But it's not true."

Maybe they were both thinking about the quote of how money doesn't buy happiness. What was the point in striving for success if people were just going to hate you?

And of course, there was her people-pleasing aspect, where she couldn't stand to have people upset with her. That complicated things at times as well. Because sometimes people just didn't like her no matter what she did.

"I suppose that's why fame and success can be such a trap. Maybe more fame or more success is what a person thinks they need when they're being shot at from below. Anything that would make them immune." He spoke thoughtfully, like he was working things out in his head.

"I agree. I think you're right about that. Or maybe people use success or money or fame or whatever as a balm to the heart pain that happens when jealous competitors take shots. It doesn't work." She could say that from experience.

"But that's not solving the problem that you have right now."

"No. It's not." She kept her chin in her hands, although she wondered what problem he thought she had, since he obviously didn't know that she couldn't cook.

Trying to figure out a way to phrase the question so he wouldn't know she was probing for details, she decided she'd just straight-out ask.

"What problem do you think I have?"

"I was hoping you would tell me."

Chapter 7

"I can't," Madeline said.

She wanted to. It was the first time she'd been tempted to share the fact that she couldn't cook with anyone other than Cheryl. But somehow sitting here and having him understand her dilemma and issues with people who were jealous of her success, and who were unkind and downright nasty doing anything to bring her down, make her look bad, just to make themselves look better, maybe that's what made her feel it was safe to share the rest.

It could ruin her career. She needed to remember that.

"My daughter's the most precious thing in the world to me." His hands moved slightly on the countertop as though admitting something so deeply profound, to him at least, made him restless. "I'm sharing her with you. Not that I have a choice," he hastened to add. "I know it's not guaranteed to work, but I'm trusting you with the most important thing in the world to me. When you said you'd help me, you didn't require anything in return. You could have." He tapped his finger on the counter. "I was just pointing that out, in case you wanted to return the favor of telling me your problem so I can offer to help with no strings attached."

He couldn't see her lips turn up, but it made her smile. He was trying to do what she did, which was give something without asking for anything in return, except he really did want something in return.

Her secret.

He wanted her secret.

"It's crazy that I'm even tempted to tell you." She couldn't even tell him how crazy it was. He could ruin her with this.

"Two things my daughter and I did together that she loved – horses and cooking. Even those haven't been enough to bridge the gap that has opened between us. I would die for her. There's nothing I wouldn't do for her. Again, I'm afraid to get my hopes up and think that it will definitely work, but it means a lot to me that you offered. Let me do something in return for you."

With those words, she suspected that he knew. At least had an idea that there was more to her and her success than what the rest of the world saw. Maybe it was just her admittedly fertile imagination.

Still, she wasn't sure she could trust him. "I don't know what to say." At least that was honest.

"Maybe you can admit what your problem is. That would be a start. And then we can brainstorm ways together and figure out how to fix it. We can do that tonight. Patty's coming tomorrow. We'll figure that out and do our best to get Lisa to leave her here, even if I have to leave the room. And then we'll go from there."

"Is Lisa going to recognize me?" The idea had just occurred to her. She was a celebrity chef after all, and her picture sometimes seemed to be everywhere, but really only people who watched cooking shows or maybe saw her on a morning news show would know her. She wasn't exactly a household name like a big A-list actor might be.

"I doubt it. I was the one who enjoyed cooking." His voice softened on the last line, almost like he didn't really want to admit it because it brought back painful memories. And again, she wondered about the fire and his hand in it.

"Will she allow Patty to stay here if she thinks I'm just, what? A random woman living with you? Am I your housekeeper?" All kinds of questions whirled through her head. They hadn't really discussed it.

"Good point. I hadn't thought of that." He shifted on the stool and put an elbow on the counter. "I guess I would have to explain why you're here. I suppose the truth would probably do, except..."

"Except why would a celebrity chef who's just using your kitchen have an interest in your daughter?"

"Exactly."

Well, she could see where this could lead—to them saying they had some kind of fake relationship. She wasn't against that, necessarily, but she didn't like lying. She had the feeling he didn't either. And then his daughter would be involved as well, and she'd already been through enough bad experiences.

"I guess I know what the obvious answer to our dilemma is, but I'm shying away from that." He didn't come right out and say that they should have a fake engagement or some kind of fake relationship, but she assumed that's what he meant.

She'd be lying if she didn't say she was a little insulted or, more likely, hurt that he didn't seem to want to do that with her. But then he explained.

"It's not that I have a problem with you, necessarily, although I understand you might have a problem with me."

She looked at him for a minute, the shape she could see outlined in the dark, anyway, considering. Finally, she decided he must be talking about his scars. What else could he mean?

Maybe it was a touchy subject, but no one ever accused her of being shy. "I suppose you mean because you think your scars make you look bad? And that somehow makes you less?"

"Don't act like you're shocked. You know it does to some people. Most people."

"Those scars were acquired when you were saving the life of your daughter, weren't they?"

Her question hung in the air between them, and he didn't answer. She could hear his breath go in and out and feel her heart pounding in her own ears, but time ticked by, and she realized he wasn't going to answer.

Why not?

She was an expert at holding up one-sided conversations though, so she dove back in.

"I guess I'm insulted that you would think that I would be in whatever group of people who care about something like that. Because no, of course it's not a shock that it does matter to some people."

"I'm sorry. I felt like I was speaking the truth, but I didn't mean to insult you."

She believed him that he didn't mean to insult her, and she tried to shove down the part of her that truly had been insulted and dredge up that part of her that knew for a fact she'd feel the exact same way if it were her face that were scarred.

"I accept your apology. And I'm sorry. I guess I just have no idea how I would handle it if I had scars that affected the way I looked." She'd always been told she was beautiful. She kind of took it for granted. Or maybe internalized it as a part of her, although she'd done nothing to deserve it.

They'd found it ironic, honestly, that Cheryl was actually the great cook, but Madeline had the personality and the looks to be in front of a camera. It made a great team, but Madeline had never really thought about what it might be like to not be comfortable having millions of people look at one.

"I don't think that's something that most people consider until it happens to them." There was a short pause. "I sure didn't. But it does. It affects everything. And suddenly just being around other people is an exercise in bravery."

"Bravery?" She felt that was a little strong. But she didn't want to judge, since she'd never been there.

"Sure. There are all different kinds of ways to show bravery. It doesn't have to be what we typically think, maybe a soldier or a hero that saves a child from being run over by a car." He hesitated a little on that last one, and she wondered again about the fire and his role in saving his daughter.

THE BEAST GETS HIS COWGIRL IN THE SHOW ME STATE

"Even if you're not concerned about how you look, there's still a certain amount of bravery that it takes to get up in front of a camera, because the potential is always there that you are going to make a fool out of yourself."

"That's true. It takes bravery to make a fool out of yourself even in front of one person, but with an audience scattered across America and the world watching, I'm sure it takes more."

He made her feel justified, because she felt like what she did wasn't easy. Especially considering that she had no idea how to cook, yet she got up in front of people all the time and acted like she did.

"I really think of myself as a brave person." She didn't mean that to brag, although as the words came out of her mouth, that's almost the way it sounded. She just meant that one didn't have to have scars in order to be brave.

He seemed thoughtful, almost pensive, and she was content to let the silence fall between them. The house was quiet, like most houses at night, and since it was newer, there wasn't even the settling and the creaking that she'd grown used to growing up in Britain in the old house there. Not to mention, with triplet sisters, even in the middle of the night, odds were that at least one of them would be awake and making noise. At any given time. She wasn't quite sure how her mother handled it, although she'd spent her fair share of time up in the middle of the night too. Not because her mother made her, but because if she heard the girls, she went to them.

All three were in the same room. She'd gotten good at making things up on the fly, entertaining them, and putting them back to sleep.

"I got the impression when you were walking in the other day that you'd never been on a working ranch before."

His voice came out of the darkness, and she felt like it was a total subject change, so it took her a little while to shift gears in her head and realize that even though what he'd said was a statement, he actually expected her to answer. She didn't have anything to hide in this area. So she shrugged.

"That's the right impression. I'm a city girl all the way. I mean it wasn't exactly the city where I grew up. In England, we all had a little garden or tiny yard in the back, and neighbors, but nothing like this. Not a barn with the house, and those the only buildings in sight. There were horses or some other animals over there inside a fence; it all looked really wonderful." She added that last bit because she'd actually loved it. She wanted to go exploring rather than going into the house and having to find the kitchen and her room. There was just something that felt like coming home when she got out of the car and looked around.

Something that had nothing to do with the way the house looked, or even the barn, but was just a feeling she got. It kind of settled on her as she twisted her head one way and then another, trying to see everything at once.

"It's funny, but when I stepped out of the car, I just felt like I was stepping out into familiar territory, even though nothing looked familiar—just the feeling I got. It's the closest feeling I've had to being home since I left England." She grunted. "This doesn't even look that much like England."

Maybe she wouldn't have admitted that much if it weren't dark. Funny how secrets had a tendency to slip out when the lights went out. And the man across from her had grown comfortable and not scary, sweet and thoughtful, and not glowering or resentful. The dark brushed away all the hard edges, and she almost felt like she could tell him anything.

"I was born and raised in this community, so I don't know what it's like to leave my home. But I know that's how I feel every time I look across the rolling hills of my part of Missouri. Like it's home, nothing else can ever compare."

She could hear the love in his voice, and the pride. Americans seemed to have a lot of that. At least throughout the different places in the heartland that she'd visited. Not so much in Hollywood.

The idea of pride in one's country was a glue that could keep a nation together. Stripping that pride away weakened the fabric of society. Maybe her distance gave her that insight.

"So you're originally from where in the United Kingdom?" he asked, taking her back just a little, because she wouldn't have thought that he was interested in her. He didn't seem like the kind of man who would ask just to make casual conversation.

"Brookshire. My mum and my three sisters are still there, although my sisters are getting ready to go to university."

"All three of them?"

"They're triplets."

"They're a lot younger than you are."

He said it is a statement, but she answered. "Yes. Twelve years. My mum had me when she was really young, and she never married my dad, who skipped out and isn't in my life. Never has been."

Pain—a little pinch—always accompanied those words.

"That's too bad."

"Yes. I guess that leaves a scar you can't see." That was all she was going to say about that. Lots of kids had their dads walk out, and she wasn't anything special in that regard. Although there would always be some part of her that wondered why he couldn't love her. Even though she knew he was young and stupid and probably scared and immature. She knew all those facts now, but as a child, all she knew was that her mum resented the fact that her dad wasn't there to help out, and her dad hadn't loved her enough to stay.

"Your mom married again."

Now he was definitely probing, and she wondered why. She didn't have the secrets that he did in his past, whatever had happened with the fire being the big one.

But she answered honestly. "No. She just wanted more children when she was established in her career, and she did in vitro fertilization using a sperm donor. I remember looking at pictures with her and even giggling over some of the descriptions. Eventually she picked a doctor with a PhD in quantum physics that looked an awful lot like Tom Cruise, only taller." Even now, the memories made her smile. That her mum had included her, that they'd gone "shopping" for a father. It had been fun.

"That's different." From his tone, she could tell he didn't see the appeal. Maybe there shouldn't have been one—a live father would definitely be better than a "shopping trip" to pick out a sperm donor. "I've never really thought about anything like that before." There was a smile in his voice, although it was hard for her to picture one on his face.

"Yeah, my mom's a little different. I probably get my quirky personality from her."

"Quirky as in getting up in the middle of the night and roaming around people's houses at all hours?"

"No. Is that quirky?" She laughed. "Quirky as in—" She waved her hand around, even though he couldn't see her, but it helped her to try to think how to describe what she meant. "—whatever personality it is that makes people like our show. That makes me be good at what I do. That makes people laugh, that makes kids like me. I don't know. Funny, in a weird way, I guess. But not so weird as to be off-putting." She added that last tastefully, lest he think that she was truly weird.

She was, but weird wasn't necessarily a compliment, and for some reason over the course of their conversation, she'd gone from thinking of him as someone she wanted to have like her because she wanted everyone to like her to thinking of him as someone she wanted to have like her because she liked him.

A development she wasn't expecting.

"Hmm. Weird and quirky and brave." His fingers tapped on the countertop again. "So I suppose I can assume since you've never been on a ranch before, you've never been around farm animals?"

"I saw cows at a petting zoo once," she said immediately. "That counts? Right?"

"Sure. That counts." His tone totally belied his words. "You've never ridden a horse?"

"Nope. I think there was a horse at that petting zoo, too. If I recall correctly, they have a kind of strong smell…actually a good smell, in a way."

"I agree with that. The horse smell is distinctive, and it's good the way the smell of leather is good. Or wood."

"Yes. Just a comforting smell. The way a mashed potato casserole is comfort food to your stomach, the horse smell is like comfort food to your soul."

"Good way to describe it. Guess I'd expect that from the…chef."

Her head snapped up at the pause that he put between what he was saying and calling her chef. It was almost like…he knew.

"So if you're brave, you'd probably enjoy riding horses tomorrow."

She had to admit her stomach had started turning at the idea that he might know her secret, because she certainly hadn't told him. It took her a little bit to get her brain to stop and focus on what he had just said. She swallowed through her tight throat. "I'd love to. Riding horses always looked like fun. But I just never had the opportunity. It's one of those things that, after I've achieved everything I want to, I'm going to learn to do."

"You can learn tomorrow morning. I'll teach you." His voice sounded almost as surprised as she felt. He was offering to teach her to ride a horse?

"You sound surprised that you even said that."

"I am." He swallowed, and she almost got the feeling that he was nervous, because his finger tapped on the countertop faster. "But I found that I really would like to. I think I would enjoy it, and I know you would. Everyone should have the opportunity to ride. Horses are great therapy animals."

"Spoken from experience?"

"I guess. For a long time, I wasn't able to ride or even work. The ranch would've gone under if it hadn't been for my brothers helping me out. But as soon as I was able, I was out. Even just brushing a horse is better than some modern-day therapy. Sometimes there's a lot to be said for the old ways."

She hadn't experienced the "old ways" much, but when she had, she'd found what he'd just said to be true. Modern ways were always touted as better, but in the long run, she'd found they seldom were. Maybe they were easier, but easier didn't mean better, not when one was looking at the long term.

Easier didn't make a person grow.

If she did easy, she wouldn't be a world-famous chef that couldn't cook.

"You haven't answered me. Does that mean you're scared? I thought you were brave."

Now it sounded like a challenge, which she probably deserved, because it had taken her longer than it should have to answer since her answer wasn't hard.

"I'd love you to teach me to ride tomorrow."

"Whoa, let me back down on the expectations. You're not going to be a professional barrel racer tomorrow after I spend two hours with you. But you might have gotten on a horse's back and ridden around the arena for a bit. If you're really lucky, you might even know how to saddle one."

She laughed. "I think I knew that much. I like you a bit more than I did at first, but I haven't decided that you're a miracle worker yet."

She could feel him still even though she couldn't see him, and she cursed her stupid mouth that always said more than it should. She didn't have to admit that she liked him.

He pushed back abruptly and stood. "You know what to expect, then. Don't expect more."

He started walking away, but she called after him, "What time?"

His footsteps didn't falter, and it didn't look like he'd turned his head. "Seven. Dress warm."

He disappeared through the dining room, with the moonlight shining on his back until he stepped into the hall and she couldn't see him any longer.

Well, even she could take that hint. She wasn't sure exactly why he'd offered to teach her to ride, but it was pretty obvious that he didn't want to have anything to do with her liking him. Maybe it was something that he offered because he was anticipating what she would do with his daughter. Probably.

Maybe she should've warned him that she wasn't a miracle worker either.

Chapter 8

Loyal didn't sleep very well. He was out at the barn by five o'clock. Dumb, because then he had two hours to think before Madeline showed up.

Usually he enjoyed his thinking time, but the only thing he seemed to be able to run over in his head was his conversation with Madeline last night.

When Chandler had first asked if Loyal could open up his home and allow a friend of Chandler's to use his kitchen, the least of his concerns was actually liking the people that were invading.

Person. Singular. The other folks didn't seem bad, but they hadn't gotten under his skin and started worming their way into his heart like Madeline had.

Not just under his skin and in his heart but also in his head, because he couldn't stop thinking about her.

He didn't typically have a problem wanting to ask people questions nor with hanging on their answers, but he was more curious than he could explain about Madeline, and he wanted to know everything.

Her childhood, and what it was like growing up in England, what her hopes and dreams were, and surprisingly, he really wanted to know what she thought about him.

Most of all, he wanted to know what he could do to get into her head the way she got into his.

"Hey there, Mama," he murmured as he went by M&M's stall. Her registered name was Missouri Mama, but her barn name was M&M, and she was due to foal anytime in the next three weeks.

Her broad forehead came across the stall, and he scratched the white blaze down her face before burying his fingers under her mane, then scratching her ears. She held still with her eyes half closed and enjoyed his ministrations.

"You like that, don't you, M&M?" He smiled as one ear flicked forward, but her eyes remained closed.

The horses had never cared about his face. They hadn't liked the smell of his bandages at first, but they'd all gotten used to them. By the time they'd come off and he'd been able to ride again, they hadn't turned an ear over the burn smell or bandages.

He only had two horses stabled inside, even though it was January. The climate in Missouri, near Cowboy Crossing, was mild enough that it didn't warrant putting them in. Even further north, they would grow heavy winter coats and be just fine outside.

But he had the room and liked to baby them if he could. Definitely M&M especially because she was so close to her foaling date.

He walked on down to the next stall and scratched the head of Cowboy Chick—barn name Chick. She and M&M were pasture buddies, and he had her in so M&M wouldn't be anxious. Horses were herd animals, and they didn't usually like to be stabled alone. Chick was bred but not due to foal until spring.

He scratched her head for a few minutes before he grabbed the wheelbarrow and started on the mucking duties.

Loyal loved the barn work, loved the silence and the animals and the comforting, familiar scents, loved using his body to get things done, even though there weren't too many things he did anymore that didn't cause him some kind of pain.

He'd not exactly been strangers with pain before the fire. Since then, he'd grown to be bedfellows with it.

He'd known almost instinctively that he'd have to put the discomfort out of his mind, and most of the time, he was successful, simply welcoming the ability to use his limbs again.

The problem with this kind of work was that it was mindless.

Normally that wasn't a problem, because he was always thinking of breeding traits for his horses, the traits of his mares that would pair well with different stallions, how to circumvent a particularly stubborn horse and get it to bend willingly to his will without its knowing what he was trying to get it to do.

Business ideas, horse ideas, constant motion in his head while he worked with his hands. Yeah, he welcomed it.

Unfortunately, Madeline had pushed all those other things aside, and he had a hard time thinking of anything but her when what he really wanted was to only think of her.

She was trouble. For him, anyway. He knew it.

Even if she weren't beautiful and vivacious and full of life, and even if she didn't seem to be his opposite in every way, she was a celebrity. Whether she belonged in Hollywood or England, it didn't really matter, because she didn't belong in rural Missouri with him and never would.

Thankfully, he hadn't fallen for her, and he wasn't going to.

Although he couldn't say exactly why he offered to teach her to ride, other than when they were talking last night, he'd remembered the wonder and eagerness that had been on her face when she'd gotten out of her car and walked to his house and how it pulled him. Her soft, wishful tones and that love of life had pulled him last night. All he could think was that he wanted to spend more time with her, give her anything he could, anything to see that smile, hear her happy voice, and have it all directed at him.

Yeah. Sometimes being in the dark with a woman made a man a fool.

He couldn't forget she was hiding a very big secret.

He'd wanted her to confide in him last night. Not even sure why. It shouldn't matter. Except, it did. He'd given her several openings, and she'd let them all go by. Obviously, she didn't trust him with her secret.

THE BEAST GETS HIS COWGIRL IN THE SHOW ME STATE

The secret that she was keeping was even more impressive considering the celebrity status that she had.

Well, impressive or what was the negative equivalent? Because basically she'd lied to everyone and gotten away with it.

How?

It had something to do with her friend, the one who wasn't here.

How was that going to play out later this week when she did her live show?

The problem wasn't his, but for some time last night, he'd wanted it to be. He'd wanted to share that burden and work on that together.

Dumb.

He'd finished feeding and had started mucking out a stall when the barn door opened and Madeline, dressed in jeans, boots, and a winter coat that looked like it belonged on TV and not in the barn, walked in, shutting the door behind her.

He liked that. The number one rule on a farm was that one closed and latched whatever one opened and unlatched. He liked that it was instinctive in her, because he'd seen a lot of people in whom it wasn't.

"Good morning." Her face beamed, and energy seemed to radiate from her. "I'm not late, am I? I thought you said seven?"

She bounded in, and the whole barn seemed to light up, the atmosphere became brighter, and he felt himself drawn toward her happiness. Or joy. Whatever it was.

He'd seen Christians who seemed to shine from within. That's the image Madeline put him to mind. Although she hadn't said anything religious that he knew of since he'd met her.

Still, it was like there was something otherworldly that shone out of her and brightened every place she was. It couldn't be Jesus though, not when she was living as big a lie as the one she was living.

He wasn't a Bible scholar, but one couldn't have iniquity in one's heart purposefully and deliberately and expect Jesus to feel welcome there too.

Which left him unable to explain why she shone with a radiance that he'd seen in very few people but greatly admired.

"I did." His mouth had finally started working to answer her question about starting at seven.

He didn't have a watch on. His phone was in his pocket, and he didn't bother to pull it out. He figured it wasn't any later than 6:30, if that.

"Okay," she said, planting her little fists on her hips and tilting her head at him. "Looks like someone should be sleeping instead of wandering around the house in the middle of the night. We get grumpy when we don't have our beauty sleep." She blinked and wiggled her brows.

His lips twitched in spite of himself. "Beauty sleep? Really?"

No one could look at him and see any kind of beauty. "There is no amount of beauty sleep that can help this," he said, referring to his face.

Loyal watched Madeline walk closer, disapproval seeming to emanate off her.

He didn't wait for her to speak. To tell him he had to get past the scar or the deformity or whatever. He didn't want to hear it coming from someone who was perfect. "You're up awfully early for someone who was up a good bit last night." He threw the pitchfork of manure in the wheelbarrow and went back in the empty stall that he'd been putting off cleaning for a while. This morning seemed like a good morning to get it done.

Right now.

"I could say the same thing about you."

Her voice was almost musical, with a good slab of humor wrapped around that English accent that should have been stiff and formal but was anything but. He'd never thought about voices or accents much before, but that was one he wouldn't mind waking up to.

He had no idea where that thought came from.

THE BEAST GETS HIS COWGIRL IN THE SHOW ME STATE

"This is the time I'm always up. It doesn't really matter how little or much sleep I get. There's always horses to feed and other chores to do, and the animals expect me to be here." He almost added that no one was going to do it for him, but he couldn't do that, because a lot of people had been doing it for him while he was recovering from the fire.

People supervised the building of his house, the breeding and foaling of his mares, and the planting and harvesting of his fields. There'd been a lot of people who helped him. He didn't want to be ungrateful.

"I see." She took several steps forward, and he set the pitchfork tongs down on the floor and leaned on it. "Are these the horses that we're riding?" She kept walking until she was in front of M&M's stall.

M&M stuck her head over, and Madeline squealed a little and jumped back.

M&M shook her head and looked like she was offended, like, "Why was the creature with the shrill voice yelling beside me?"

Loyal tried to bite back a smile—he did that a lot around Madeline. He wouldn't have thought he'd think it was cute for her to squeal over the horse, but she was just so adorable.

When was the last time he thought of a woman as adorable?

She probably wouldn't consider that a compliment, either. But she was, and even now, before he'd said anything, she was inching closer to the horse she'd just jumped from.

"I'm assuming that if this horse was going to attack and eat me, you would've said something." She slid her eyes to him, keeping her body squared with the horse. "Is that a bad assumption?"

Again, he had to work to keep his lips from twitching up from the humorous way she asked that question.

"I'm pretty sure you signed a nonliability statement, agreeing to hold me harmless for any accidents or injuries that you receive while you're here on my property. So, technically, it's no skin off my back whether you get attacked or not."

This time when she slanted her eyes over, they were narrowed. Loyal had the feeling she would have crossed her arms over her chest, except she didn't want to move and scare the horse...into attacking her maybe?

She tilted her head a little. "So I have to worry about being attacked?" She lifted her nose, looked at the horse, and gave a very little, very English, sniff.

Heaven help him, but his lip did more than twitch that time. It curved a little, and he couldn't stop it.

"I think it would be messy if I allowed her to attack you right here in the barn."

"Oh, most definitely. Because I'll be going after that pitchfork you're leaning on. Things definitely would get messy."

That time, both of his lips wanted to turn up. "You don't really look like a pitchfork-wielding person." She didn't sound like one, either.

"I have a lot of experience with knives. Sharp things. I think I can make a pitchfork do what I want it to do. Especially if it will keep me from being killed." She turned to face the horse full-on.

He highly suspected that she wouldn't have it in her to hurt a horse, no matter what the horse was doing to her, and he thought that her words were probably just that. Words.

But he couldn't seem to stop himself from teasing her. "Maybe that's my prized horse, and maybe I would fight you for this pitchfork."

This time, there was a definite twinkle in her eyes when she slanted them over to him. "I highly doubt that."

His brow shot up. "Really?"

She gave a decisive nod. "Really."

"Do you care to explain?" It was a question, but he really meant it as a demand.

She didn't quibble over the details. Her mouth opened immediately. "Of course. You're not going to win that fight."

"A beauty contest, you win. A wrestling match over the pitchfork, it's me, all day long."

THE BEAST GETS HIS COWGIRL IN THE SHOW ME STATE 75

She harrumphed. "Not so."

"Maybe you've missed it, but I'm bigger than you are. By a lot. I'll win."

"No. You won't. Because you might be bigger, but you also subscribe to that whole ladies first, open the door for a lady, and, in this case, the applicable one is you won't hit a lady." She wiggled her fingers at him. "I fight dirty."

"You do." He nodded. She was right. He wouldn't fight her. Not a hitting fight.

Although, he was pretty sure they were joking.

She gave a triumphant smile, and he let her think for a couple of seconds that she won.

After a long pause, he said, "The whole argument is moot, because you would never use a pitchfork on the horse anyway."

Her smile froze on her face before it turned into a sheepish grin. "Busted." She lifted her shoulder. "You're right. If she charged me, I would be running. And since I'm pretty sure that a quarter horse can outrun me, I'll be looking for something to climb." She pursed her lips and threw a glance at him. "Horses don't climb, correct?"

It was a teasing question that probably had a hint of seriousness to it. After all, she'd admitted she knew nothing about farm animals in general and horses in particular. He had a mind to tease her, but he didn't.

Not really. "You know, as a farmer, you have the tendency to see it all. And to think you've seen it all." He tapped the pitchfork on the floor thoughtfully. "Then one day, you see something you've never seen before, and you realize you really haven't seen it all. I kinda figured that's the way the rest of my life is going to go. Periods of thinking that I know it all followed by the assurance that I absolutely do not."

"Spoken like you've had some experience." It came out as a comment, but her voice ended on a high note, like she might be asking a question.

He indulged.

"One time, I came upon one of my horses: half of her was on one side of the gate, her body went through the gate, and half of her was on the other side. I have no idea how she managed to get herself in there. It was way too small for her to get in or out, either way. In fact, in order to get her out, we had to take the welder and cut the bar off the gate."

"Sounds like that was an interesting day."

"Sure was. As a farmer, we get a lot of those."

Her expression said she understood. "I don't know much about farming, but I do know that in my business, it's people that surprise you. You think you know what they're going to do, then you find out you were wrong, and you really didn't know anything."

He thought of her secret and the fact that she didn't know that he knew, and he wondered if that was what she was talking about.

"A lot of times, they say they're going to do things, and they don't. They make promises they don't keep. They pretend you're their friend, just so they can get ahead. I guess we talked about it a little bit, and I just came to that conclusion—rather like you—there's nothing you're going to do about it." Most of the sparkle had gone out of her eyes, and he figured she'd been hurt by people just as she'd said.

Then her chin came up. "I won't allow myself to get bitter over it. Because I'm not going to be a bitter person." She lifted a shoulder, and he had the feeling that the smile that she gave was one that she forced on her face, which was the first such smile he'd seen. Normally, her lips lifted easily and freely. "I'm not going to withdraw or get hard or cynical. I'm going to keep getting up and going out and loving freely, giving kindness liberally, and trusting without reservation."

He didn't really think that she was hitting him. It just seemed to be a natural turn of the conversation and an issue that she'd struggled with, maybe.

But he had issues with everything she said. He knew he did. Who wouldn't, if they looked like him? Because, yeah, he was bitter.

Bitter about the fire. Bitter about his wife. Bitter about the fact that his daughter screamed every time she saw him. And, of course, bitter about the fact that he'd been burned, and he had to live with scars the rest of his life, while his wife seemed to have gotten off completely free, even though she was the one who was committing adultery while their house burned down and their son died.

Bitter at God. Yeah. Most definitely.

"Hey. You seem to have wandered off there for a bit."

He turned his head, realizing that Madeline was peering at him and that wasn't the first thing she'd said that he hadn't heard.

"I'm sorry. Since you're out here, we might as well start your riding lessons." He walked the pitchfork over to the corner and hung it on the nails on the wall.

He'd changed the subject abruptly, and he wasn't giving an explanation for it. He turned back around, ready to deflect or outright ignore any questions or probing she wanted to do.

"This is the horse I'm riding?" she asked, allowing the subject change easily, as though she knew maybe he needed it. Because he wasn't ready to go where he'd gone in his head out loud.

He didn't want to spend the rest of his life bitter either.

He definitely didn't want to spend it bitter at God.

But he wasn't really sure what to do about it. Because after all, if God was totally in control of everything, then God allowed his child to die, allowed him to be scarred, allowed him to lose the precious relationship he'd had with his daughter, and allowed his wife to get away with absolutely no punishment.

"No. That's M&M."

"M&M, like the candy?"

"No. Well, yeah. I guess." He needed to pull his head out from the memories and the guilt over his inability to not be bitter.

He walked over to the stall. "Her registered name is Missouri Mama. But her barn name, which is just a horse term for nickname, is M&M."

It was funny, but he never, ever forgot his scars. They were always front and center in his mind anytime he went anywhere or talked to anyone.

Except when he spoke to Madeline. She had a way of making him forget. Treating him like she didn't notice it or didn't care, or maybe it was more the way she made him feel.

Normally the scars made him feel less, or ugly, or somehow not as good, and yet she laughed and joked and treated him like he was normal, like she liked him. Despite the fact that he knew that he didn't always act in the most becoming way.

Maybe that was another thing; she seemed to bring out the good in him.

He wanted to think about that one later, because it felt like a bold thought. The kind of thought that made perfect sense now that he thought about it. Madeline made him better. Being around her, talking to her, working with her, just sitting in the kitchen in the dark with her made him better. Or made him want to be better.

No wonder he felt pulled toward her.

"So...are you still thinking about which horse I'm going to ride, or did you space out on me again?" She tilted her head, and it was on the tip of his tongue to tell her that she looked adorable when she looked at him like that, but thankfully his common sense hadn't completely left the room, and he was able to clamp his teeth around his tongue and keep those words from slipping out.

"The horse you're gonna ride is outside. You have to go get her." It was his turn to give her a challenging look.

She crossed her arms over her chest and tapped her toe. "Is part of the lesson going to be you teaching me how to go get the horse, or is this the part of the lesson that I have to Google?"

"Google? You're serious?" There his lips went tilting up again, and he'd lost the heart to even try to stop them. How long had it been since he'd enjoyed teasing someone like this?

She pressed her lips together, which didn't disguise the twinkle in her eyes, before she fished around her back pocket and pulled her phone out. "I'll do what any modern woman would do. I'll ask Siri."

He was hard-pressed not to giggle over that one. Or chuckle. Chuckling was more manly than giggling. "Go ahead. We'll see what Siri says about going out and catching your horse."

She did a few things on her phone, then held it up to her lips. "Siri, how do I walk out to the field and catch a horse."

"Here's what I found on the web about 'how do I walk out to the field and catch a horse.'"

"That was helpful."

He leaned forward, trying to peer over the top of her phone and read it upside down, curious as to what exactly Siri had found on the web. He started to read, "If you go out into the pasture passively with your hands closed, your horse should come to you." He grunted. "Hmm. Interesting."

"Okay," Madeline said as she scrolled down. "Some ads on lead ropes, a video on planting the right type of pasture seed, and an article on how to use a lasso. Obviously, I'm going to have to go with plan B. Because plan A was a bust."

"What's plan B?"

"For being the teacher today, you're asking an awful lot of questions." She put one hand on her hip and shoved her phone in her back pocket with the other.

"I think I read somewhere that a good teacher asks questions that stimulate critical thinking."

"Not when the teacher is supposed to be teaching the student how to ride a horse. I don't need to critically think, I just need a horse."

He shook his head in mock consternation. "That's the trouble with the world today. Everybody wants everybody else to do everything for them."

"Fine. I can call your brother. I'm on a first-name basis with him. Maybe he'll come over and show me how to catch a horse. That's plan C."

He laughed. "If you're talking about Chandler, you probably ought to wait at least five or six hours. He's on Hollywood time, and he won't be out of bed until, oh, roundabout noon thirty." That was a total lie. Chandler and Ivory had been working their own spread for a while, and Chandler was probably out feeding his animals right now. But he definitely didn't want Madeline calling his brother. He wanted to take care of her himself. He just wanted to tease her a little first.

Speaking of teasing her, he just had a really great idea. "Tell you what. I'll stop asking you questions, won't ask you another thing, if you trade me horse riding lessons for cooking lessons."

He had no idea why he couldn't stop testing her like this. He wanted her to tell him her secret. Although he had no right and no reason to expect her to feel like she could confide in him.

Her face dimmed ever so slightly—he wouldn't have noticed it if he hadn't been watching for it. Then she gave him a jaunty smile.

"So what I'll do is take you into the kitchen and tell you to ask Siri to find the ingredients and the recipe and to show you how to make it." She grinned at him, and he found himself grinning back, without even thinking about it, even though there was a part of him that was disappointed that she'd had an opportunity to trust him and had let it go by again. He knew he was being ridiculous to even hope that she would. She barely knew him.

"I suppose that's fair," he said. "So, if I show you step-by-step how to not only ride the horse but to catch her and saddle her, then you'll do the same for me in the kitchen?"

THE BEAST GETS HIS COWGIRL IN THE SHOW ME STATE 81

Her eyes narrowed just a touch, almost like she was wondering if he knew more than she thought he did. His grin held, and he met her eyes second by second. Part of him wanted her to call him out, and part of him wanted her to break down.

There was also a part of him that surprised him, because that part was the stronger part, and it wanted to protect her.

"That sounds like it might be a fair exchange, except you are the one with a world-class kitchen, and you're the one whom I was told was an amateur chef. Apparently, it's something you do in your spare time? So why would you need me to teach you anything?" Her lips pursed, and her eyes twinkled, like maybe she suspected that he had knowledge that she hadn't thought he had, and she was challenging him. Or maybe it was just the way she was.

"Anyone with an accent like you have has got to be able to show me something. I'm just a cowboy from rural America. You sound like you've been all over the world." He grabbed the bucket and slapped a little feed into it. "When we walk out, the horses will come to us, wanting the feed. Makes it a lot easier to catch them. I already fed them this morning, and I only grain them in the evening. This is a treat."

Chapter 9

"Oh. I see." Madeline watched with interest as he gathered the stuff up.

He motioned for her, and she followed him out a different door than the one she came in through. He led her to a fenced enclosure that maybe was a corral, but she wasn't sure, and he didn't say, where five or six horses ate hay off the ground.

He set everything he brought out down. "Can you climb over the fence?" He didn't wait for her to answer but put a foot on the bottom slats, stepped up, and swung a leg over.

She could do that. She was a little more awkward than he was but not too bad considering she'd never done it before.

"Is there a reason you're not using the gate?" she asked, only a little jokingly.

"Just wanted to see if you could climb over the fence," he said, and she thought that might have been a wink, but she couldn't see his eyes very well under his cowboy hat.

"All right, when you're around horses, you want to walk slowly and speak softly. You don't have to be afraid of them, but you do want to keep from scaring them, so no sudden movements, and you don't want to yell unless it's an emergency."

He almost became a different person when he started working with his horses. It was like he forgot about the scars on his face and spoke with confidence and moved the same way.

She nodded, even though he couldn't see her, and followed him.

As he caught the horse and snapped a lead on her which she hadn't even seen until he did it, he explained what he was doing in a low tone that she supposed was informative for her and designed to soothe the horse as well.

She liked the tone. It wasn't exactly provocative, but it felt like chocolate in her heart, and she felt like she could listen to it for hours and hours.

He had her hold her hand out so the horse could sniff her. She petted her some, and then he brushed her and tacked her up as he explained each step as he did it.

"I know I'm not going to be able to remember all of this for next time."

"Next time, we'll have you doing some, but I'll still be helping you. I know that you're not gonna learn this in one lesson."

She appreciated that and stopped worrying about hanging on his every single syllable, but just enjoyed listening and watching him. The horse was pretty too. With the big blotch of white surrounded by red and a red mane and a tail that was both red and white. She wasn't sure exactly what color combination that was called, but it was pretty.

"Now I'll hold her, and you can put a foot in the stirrup and pull yourself into the saddle, if you're comfortable." He looked at her, assessing, and she held his eyes for a minute before she turned to look at the horse. She wasn't afraid, exactly. Maybe a little uncertain.

Loyal wasn't going to ask her to do something that he thought was going to hurt her. She knew that as sure as she knew her own name. Just after watching him with the horse, and the gentleness with which he held her and handled her, and the consideration he showed as he went through the steps, maybe it was all designed to earn the horse's trust, but he'd earned hers as well. If he hadn't already had it.

"I trust you," she said.

Moving closer to the horse, she touched her neck before she put a hand on the stirrup and lifted her right foot up.

Loyal seemed to shift beside her and then pause, which made her look at him.

"How do you think that's gonna work?" he asked, nodding at her foot in the stirrup.

It took her a couple seconds before she realized that she'd be stepping up with her right foot, and if she swung her left leg over, she'd end up backwards on the saddle.

"Okay. You mount on the left side and use your left foot first. That feels a little unnatural, but I can see it makes sense."

His teeth flashed, and it was a natural smile, like he forgot about scars and all the things that he seemed to carry around like a chip on his shoulder when they were in the house together. She liked this new, softer, more natural side of him, like he wasn't concerned about his looks or her status and they were just equals, with him teaching her and being considerate and kind and her listening and learning and making him smile.

She switched feet, and it was a little harder than she had thought because it was big step, but she was able to pull herself up, throw the right leg over, and plop down in the saddle.

He hadn't moved to hand her the reins when a little boy came into her peripheral vision, leaning on the fence by the gate.

Madeline wanted to look at him, ask who he was and what he needed—he looked a little ragged, and her first instinct was to feed him—but she was sitting on something that was moving. Even though it wasn't moving forward, it was moving under her by centimeters or inches, swaying back and forth, and her new perspective seemed very, very high.

She'd never considered herself afraid of heights, but her hands clenched on the rough strands of the mane in front of her, and her feet knocked against the sides of the horse, which seemed to make the horse prance even more.

Her stomach tilted and shifted as though it wanted to get off the horse, and her throat was suddenly dry.

The little boy said something, but by this time, Madeline's heart was flopping like a hummingbird's wing in her throat, and she had both lips pulled in and clinched down tight with her teeth; otherwise, she'd have been begging Loyal to get her down.

Now.

Loyal spoke low, and she thought he might be talking to the horse, because his hand went to its neck, stroking.

Without unclenching her teeth, she tried to take a deep breath through her nose. Surely if she were going to die, he would be a little more upset. But she hadn't expected to feel so...exposed, high, completely out of control. She wasn't used to her seat moving, even though it wasn't moving very much.

Why couldn't the horse just stand still?

"I think you're going to make your lips bleed if you keep biting down on them like that. Are you that scared?" Loyal spoke softly and calmly beside her. One hand on the horse's neck. One hand still holding the reins.

Her head automatically started to shake in denial before she stopped it, then gave a reluctant nod.

"I'm scared. I wasn't expecting to be high and moving, and everything feels like I'm about to fall off at any second."

"Do you want me to help you back down?" Again, his voice was soft and low. Not quite a whisper, but it wouldn't carry even to the fence where the little boy still stood.

Her fingers tightened in the mane, and although she wanted to say *yes, please get me out of here*, she didn't like to give up. She wasn't good at it, and there weren't too many times in her life where she had.

Whether he noticed the tightening of her hands, or whether it was just a natural thing, his hand moved from the horse's neck and covered hers.

Immediately, she felt better. Not perfect, and the fear didn't go away, but over the fear, confidence seemed to settle.

She would be okay.

He wouldn't let anything happen to her.

She wanted to turn her hand over, and thread her fingers with his, and squeeze as tight as she could. Something told her that all that would only make her feel better.

Her muscles still tensed painfully, and her jaw clenched, but she felt like she was able to shift her eyes slightly, and they met his, concerned and dark and looking up at her. The touch of his eyes was almost as strong as the physical touch of his hand and just as calming. There were eddies and swirls in a deep pool, and the back of her neck relaxed, and warmth flowed down her backbone and out her arms.

Maybe the horse felt her new calmness, because it stopped moving underneath her, although she barely noticed.

Maybe the horse stomped the ground, but something shifted, and the friction of his hand sliding over hers almost produced sparks. It wouldn't have shocked her to see bright lights flashing.

Her eyes widened; she couldn't stop them.

His did too, for a fraction of a second, before they narrowed, and some other emotion flowed over his face. Maybe determination, maybe disgust.

Whatever it was, his hand disappeared from hers, and he moved in front of the horse.

"Teddy. How did you know we were riding? You always come at the right time." His voice held that note that adults' voices often did when they spoke with children. A combination of easy familiarity and cuteness.

The boy's shoulders went up and down, and he smiled, his teeth big in his face and slightly crooked.

If Madeline had been on the ground, she would have grinned back at the boy and started up a conversation with him. He looked cute and sweet and innocent, but there was also wariness and a tension in the way he held himself. Something about the glances he threw around, the way his hands clutched the boards, told her that maybe his home life wasn't the best.

She was making a wild assumption, but she'd seen looks like his before, and it was a gut feeling.

It helped her to forget about where she was, thinking about what she could do to help him.

They donated a lot of food from their show, and immediately she thought of giving some to him. Despite all the practicing she'd done, she didn't really have anything that was edible.

She could do hot chocolate though.

But she kept her mouth shut, because she wasn't sure how Loyal would feel about her inviting the little boy into his kitchen to make hot chocolate for him. It wasn't exactly hers to offer.

She didn't have to wonder long.

"Want me to saddle someone up for you?" Loyal asked in the same low tone he'd been using the whole time while looking over at Teddy.

"Can I try to do it myself?" The little boy's voice held that squeak and just a hint of a rumble that boys' voices often did as they changed from child to man. It probably made the kid older than what Madeline had originally thought, but maybe he was small for his age.

"You sure can. Come on in here, and you can grab Badger."

Madeline's torso spasmed as she worried that Loyal would let go of her horse and go off with the little boy, but she gradually relaxed as Loyal just watched. The boy grabbed a lead rope and walked into the group of horses, talking softly, as she assumed he'd been taught to do by Loyal, and hooking onto the face straps—whatever those things on their faces were called—of the brown horse she assumed was Badger.

"That's a halter." Loyal looked up at her, his eyes twinkling, the self-consciousness still gone. His gaze was as magnetic as it had been the last time they'd looked at each other.

It made her forget she was sitting on a horse and uncomfortable and scared. It made her forget about the scruffy-looking little boy that pulled at her heart and made her want to learn to cook just so she could feed him. Forget about the cold, forget about the fact that her TV show and best friend's and her entire fortune was on the line. All she wanted to do was sink deeper into that perceptive gaze.

She shook herself and looked away.

Perceptive.

When she looked at him, she felt like he knew her secrets. She didn't feel judged, but she definitely did feel like he knew more than she thought he did and almost got the impression that he wanted her to tell him. Confide.

She'd heard from other people that horses were a form of therapy, and she almost would think that was true with the way she was reacting to Loyal.

Although she couldn't blame the horse entirely. The hypnotizing way Loyal walked, slow and steady but with determination and purpose, around them and the low tones he used were hypnotic and pulled at her.

The gentleness, the consideration, the calm confidence, and his total lack of self-consciousness of his scars that had not dropped for an instant when they'd been in the house. It all pulled her.

Horses might be therapeutic, but that didn't explain her attraction to Loyal.

"Are you ready to walk?"

She nodded, then licked her dry lips, staring between the horse's ears. "I think so. But I'm not ready to steer it myself yet."

He laughed. "Teddy's gonna tie Badger up to the fence, then he'll be going in for his tack. He should be able to tack him up himself, although I'll be there to give him a hand. While we're waiting on that, I'll take you for a short walk if you're good for it."

"Thank you for taking it slow. This is completely new and more than a little scary." She felt a little bit like a baby and slightly embarrassed. She'd been finding so much in him to admire, and here she was practically shaking on top of the gentlest horse he owned and being completely needy and dependent.

Hardly a desirable woman.

Plus, even if he did find something to admire, it was all going to blow up as soon as she got in front of the live cameras. There was absolutely no point in going there.

"We all start somewhere."

"So you were like this when you first learned to ride?"

He lifted his shoulder. "Maybe. I was probably too young and dumb to be scared. I was riding before I could walk. I have baby pictures of my mom holding me on a horse."

"She must be quite a woman. She had a baby, and she was still riding horses. I'd be way too scared."

"I think she was pretty much the perfect farmer's wife." He seemed to think for a minute. "I don't know if I've ever seen my mom scared."

He said that with a little bit of color in his tone, like he was remembering, and she wondered if it had something to do with the fire and possibly the loss of his child or the fact that he'd been in the hospital and perhaps his life was hanging precariously for a while.

"I don't think anyone who knows me could say that about me. That's a pretty big compliment coming from her son—that she'd never been scared."

"I didn't say she's never been scared. I just said I've never seen her scared. I'm sure she's felt fear, but her faith has always been bigger. And she's the best person I know with putting boots on that faith and taking it out into life with her."

His words made Madeline curious to meet his mom. She'd never in her life met someone who talked about their mother that way. Funny, when folks lived together as a family, they saw everything, and somehow, the faults always seemed to loom larger than the virtues.

Her mum had been overwhelmed bringing three babies home. Overwhelmed raising them. Overwhelmed working and being a single mom. There might have been faith there, but Madeline couldn't look back and say that she really saw it. Maybe the difference was her perception of her mum versus Loyal's perception of his. Maybe he was just better at seeing the good in people.

She glanced sideways at him, interested to see this side of him, the side that worked with horses and was gentle and sweet and spoke highly of his mother. It certainly was not a side she'd been expecting.

A little buzzing in the distance grew louder and louder until it took her attention away from Loyal and made her look up to the sky.

By that time, it felt like the ground had started to shake. Her horse sidestepped nervously. Her heart lurched. She grabbed at the mane, her fingers clutching. The sound grew louder.

"Whoa," Loyal said as Missy pranced. "It's a fighter jet. They don't go by often. Hold on."

He said that in the same tone he'd been talking to the horse, but she assumed he was reassuring her. It worked until Teddy yelled.

Her head whipped around, and she saw the little boy holding a saddle and standing inside the fence. The horse that he'd tied had moved around, not quite pinning him against the boards.

As though the loud voice had scared Missy as much as the fighter jet which had grown even louder, she shook her head and shied to the side as the noise became deafening.

Loyal's attention had been on Teddy. The reins slid out of his hand. Madeline's hands had loosened some with Loyal's assurance, but she grabbed tighter now.

The horse slid out from underneath her. She was able to hold on. Barely.

But when Missy took two running steps, then swerved away from the fence, Madeline was jerked from one side to the other and couldn't hang on. Her body slipped out of the saddle. Her head cracked against the fence before she flopped onto the ground with a thud.

"Madeline!"

Chapter 10

She heard Loyal's voice from a distance but couldn't get air in her lungs to answer him.

Her head hurt, and it felt like there was something wet on it. She thought maybe she was bleeding from hitting her head on the fence, but she couldn't get her arm to move to touch it.

For what felt like long minutes but was probably only a few seconds, all she could do was lie and stare at the sky, bright blue and completely empty.

The jet was gone, the noise fading away, and though the horses shuffled around the enclosure nervously, things had calmed.

Fingers skimmed along her temple, and her eyes, seeming to only obey her slowly, moved to see Loyal's head bend above her. It was fuzzy, and at times, there seemed to be two of him.

"Teddy?" she managed to croak out, hoping he understood what she was asking with one word.

"He's fine."

As though to prove the point, a second head appeared over Loyal's shoulder, eyes blinking, brows knotted, and concern clouding the little features.

"Is she dead?" he whispered in a slightly awed tone, as though he didn't want to speak too loud in the presence of a corpse.

She had to answer that one. "No."

She blinked her eyes twice just in case he didn't believe her, still not feeling like she wanted to move, although her breath was coming a little easier.

"I'm gonna touch your head to try to stop the bleeding," Loyal said before he produced a rag from somewhere and touched it to the area just above her ear.

She flinched. It hurt. Pinching pain, but also giving her an ugly feeling in her stomach like there just wasn't something quite right with her body, and things didn't sit right.

"Head wounds usually bleed a lot, as this one's doing. I think we'll find it's probably not as bad as it seems." Loyal's voice was confident, but there was a shadow of the past over his eyes, like he was hoping his words were true but wasn't as entirely sure as he sounded.

Madeline closed her eyes. She wished she hadn't seen that uncertainty. It fueled her own. Except, she was pretty sure she was okay.

"As soon as I can breathe again normally, I think I'll be fine. There's no pain." No pain that felt sharp and dangerous at least.

There was a little bit of throbbing, because one didn't fall and hit the ground the way she had and not feel *something*.

"I fell off a horse before. It hurts." Teddy looked at her, his eyes uncertain, like he didn't know whether to admire her because she wasn't in pain or to be worried about her.

"I agree. It does hurt. I meant I don't think I have any broken bones or internal injuries. But yes, my butt hurts."

Teddy smiled at that, then giggled.

Madeline smiled at the boy. Then as her eyes were sliding off him, they hooked on Loyal's gaze.

She'd lost count of the number of times she'd gotten trapped in his eyes that morning. Way too many. Of course, there wasn't too much she could do about it right now, lying prone as she was and still not able to take a deep breath.

She was pretty sure her lungs just got shook up though.

"We'll see if you can move your arms and legs first. Don't try to sit up. If you do have some kind of back injury, you're not supposed to move. But I don't think we need to get too crazy, because you really did hit butt first after you smacked your head on the fence." Loyal was looking at her with an assessing gaze, his eyes moving over her head and down her limbs as though making sure as he spoke that he wasn't missing anything.

Her lungs had finally stopped spasming, and her breath, though shaky, felt more natural. She lifted a hand and then another one. "I think these are working well."

"That's good because I'm hungry." His eyes held humor, and possibly, was that a challenge in them?

"Me too. Does Madeline cook good?" Teddy asked.

"She sure does. She has her own cooking show on TV. Don't you recognize her?" Now Loyal really was joking, and he wasn't trying to hide the smile on his face. She wasn't sure if he was laughing at her or with Teddy. Maybe the knock on her head had addled her brains more than she thought.

Teddy scrunched up his face as he gazed down at her. "My gram watches cooking shows sometimes. And there's someone that talks weird like you do on them." He wrinkled his nose. "She usually has her hair brushed."

Madeline wanted to smile and sink into the ground at the same time. But she said, "And she probably doesn't have a bloodied rag stuck to her forehead either?"

Teddy nodded thoughtfully. He'd taken her question seriously. "No. No blood on the cooking shows. My gram wouldn't watch them if there were. She hates blood. I had to put my own bandages on back when I was kid and wore them."

Madeline tried to keep her lips from turning up. She caught Loyal having the same problem, and they shared a smile with their eyes only.

But then she blinked and looked away. She had to remember what was going to be happening this week and not let her guard down. Not to mention, she was pretty sure what she was feeling was a lot different than what the man beside her was. She had done nothing but look incompetent pretty much from the second she got here. There was no way he could be interested in her.

"Wiggling my toes. Bending my knees. Lifting my legs." She lifted her brows at him. "I think I'm good. Ready to sit up." She was tired of lying around being helpless and ready to do something she was good at.

Hopefully no one asked her to cook breakfast.

"Do it slowly. Let me know if you're feeling any pain anywhere except your head," he said, leaning back but not moving away.

Madeline obeyed, moving slowly into a sitting position, then pausing there with her legs bent and one arm around her knees.

Loyal continued to press on the rag. "Your head is still bleeding. I think we can get you into the house, and it'd be good for you to lie down for a bit, although I'm pretty sure you shouldn't fall asleep." He tilted his head. "Unless you want to go to the emergency room?" He sounded almost hopeful, like he hoped she would.

"I just bumped my head, and it's bleeding. There's no need for me to go to the ER." That was the truth. There wasn't anything wrong with her other than she had the wind knocked out of her, and she had some kind of cut on her head. "Unless you don't want to bother with me in your house, and you'd rather dump me off for them to deal with. I'm fine with that." She didn't want to be a bother, any more than what she had been. He hadn't really signed up for this. "Although don't forget Lisa's coming."

His eyes widened, like he had totally forgotten that, and she watched as awareness crept back into them, and he moved his head slightly, tilting it out of the way so his good side was toward her. The knowledge of his scars had settled back down.

She hated that. She'd really liked that he'd seemed to almost trust her when he'd forgotten about them. It was probably more about the horses than her. Still. She liked the natural, unaffected Loyal much better than the one who was ashamed and embarrassed about his face.

It made her heart twist in an uncomfortable and almost painful way.

"Teddy, do you think you can take Missy's tack off her and brush her down? I don't think we're going to do any more riding today."

"Yes sir." Teddy got up and started to walk away before he turned back around. "I thought you told me that if you fall off a horse, you need to get right back on?"

Loyal nodded, his eyes as serious as ever. "And I believe that. But if you're bleeding, there might be an exception. Possibly an exception for broken bones as well."

His eyes skittered to hers, and Madeline felt the shock as they met again, his filled with compassion and concern, despite the distance that he put between them as he shifted away from her.

"Actually, I think I should carry you in. You probably shouldn't be very active with this much blood gushing out of that wound. Not to mention, after that hit, you might be dizzy."

Madeline shook her head, making the world spin, even though she was still sitting down, and throwing stabs of pain from one side of her skull to the other. Maybe she should let him carry her.

She didn't really want to, though. Didn't want to touch him, didn't want to be close to him. She'd already been admiring him way too much.

Admiration was one thing, but adding in the feelings that had been turning in her heart as well as the attraction that she was having trouble denying, and it was almost enough to talk a girl into going to the hospital.

Except she didn't want to do that either. The last thing she needed was for that to hit the press, although she was ashamed to admit for a second she thought about using this as an excuse to get out of the live show, or she could at least use it as a reason if she didn't do well when...she didn't do well.

But that wouldn't be taking responsibility for her actions, and it would be lying, and she wouldn't like the person she was if she did that. So, as tempting as that might be, she shoved those thoughts out of her head.

"Let me stand up and see how I feel."

Loyal's lips pressed together, but he moved back as her fingers replaced his holding the rag to her head. It was wet, and honestly, she was surprised at the amount of blood she'd lost. It scared her a bit too. But she also, for some odd reason, trusted Loyal, and he said he didn't think there was anything to worry about.

She could go with that.

"You have a lot of brothers, don't you?" she asked as she pushed off from the ground.

"Five. Why?"

"I assume you have experience in head wounds. Boys seem to encounter that type of thing more than girls."

He humphed. "I guess you're right. But yeah, we hit our heads and bled like stuck pigs all the time growing up. This is totally normal. But I do want to take a look at it once you're settled. I'll be able to tell when I see it whether you should go get stitches or not."

"I really don't want to go to the hospital. The media will be all over that, and it will be bad press," she said softly as she gathered herself to push off the ground. One foot solid, balancing on her other knee, until she felt steady enough to rise.

"We'll see if we can't do it quietly if we need to. I know a few people who know a few people."

That made her eyes shoot to his. "You make it sound like you're a member of the Mafia."

His lips turned up, and his eyes crinkled. "I have the looks for it, don't I?"

THE BEAST GETS HIS COWGIRL IN THE SHOW ME STATE

She shook her head. "You have those chocolate eyes and that little-boy smile. You don't look anything like a member of the mob. Maybe a Boy Scout."

Maybe her smile was a little wan, but even she could hear the warmth in her words. Warmth that was probably inappropriate and definitely crossed the line that she'd drawn for herself. She couldn't help it. His eyes reminded her of chocolate, or rich wood, or expensive leather.

But she'd said way too much, or maybe her tone had said way too much.

His eyes widened, and his mouth opened and closed, and she didn't look to see more but put her eyes on the ground and pushed up.

The world spun, and her hands went flying—one grabbing the fence and one smacking into Loyal's chest. A second later, he scooped her up.

"That's what I thought. That was a pretty hard hit. Push harder on the rag. Your wound started gushing again."

She pushed harder, closing her eyes. Half because of the dizziness, half because of embarrassment.

In her work, she'd met all kinds of men but never anyone like Loyal.

In her life, she didn't think that she'd probably looked worse in front of anyone. Which was too bad, because Loyal was the kind of man a girl could fall in love with.

Chapter 11

Loyal held Madeline in his arms and watched with concern as her eyes closed and her forehead wrinkled.

Maybe he should say she should go to the emergency room. Maybe he shouldn't be so blasé just because he and his brothers had survived countless head wounds like this. They all had scars on their heads from falling. It was part of life. And yeah, he knew about concussions, and they weren't good, and they could have lifelong consequences, but he also found it crazy to put restrictions on everything just because a person was afraid of getting hurt.

A personal opinion he and his brothers all shared but wasn't popular in the rest of the world. So he kept his mouth shut and wondered if he shouldn't do something that he normally wouldn't with a woman in his arms.

Maybe she'd have been able to stand. He'd been quick to scoop her up. He'd offered, only half thinking she needed him to; the other half of him had wanted to.

She hadn't wanted to stay on the horse. She'd been scared. He admired the fact that she shoved her fear aside and faced the things she didn't want to do head-on with a determination that had impressed him. But he also felt guilty that she'd trusted him to keep her safe and he'd let her down.

Not on purpose, of course, but he wouldn't blame her if she didn't trust him again.

Some people took to riding horses like it was a natural thing, and other people never felt natural on a horse, usually giving up. One typically either loved it or didn't. Madeline was one of those for whom, if she ever did ride, it wouldn't be a natural thing. He could tell that much from just watching her.

But he'd seen a lot of people give up over less, and she hadn't begged to get off or even suggested it. She had trusted him.

Maybe it was the trust that she'd placed in him that had made him try to rise to the occasion to deserve what she'd given him and be the man she was assuming he was, instead of the man he knew himself to be.

People could change and grow. He believed that. He'd seen it in his own life.

And people could be inspired to change and grow. Those were the kind of feelings that were stirring in his chest as Madeline turned still-trusting eyes on him, and looked at him like he was more than a scarred and broken cowboy, and treated him like he deserved to have her trusting him and to be teaching her.

Her eyes closed.

"Are you tired, resting your eyes, or did you pass out?" he asked, pretty sure she hadn't passed out, and he knew she hadn't fallen asleep.

Really, what he wanted was to look into those emerald green eyes again. Every time he looked at her, something tugged inside of him. He hadn't figured out what it was, but she made him feel warm and good and better in a way he couldn't explain.

Maybe it was the expression on her face as she looked at him. Truly looked at him.

His scars didn't seem to bother her or make him look less. In fact, she didn't really seem to see his physical self at all. At least that's the impression he got when their eyes met and held. It was more like she saw inside of him. Maybe she saw the bad and the good and chose to focus on the good. Or chose to focus on what he could be; even as she made him feel like he was perfect the way he was, he wanted to strive to be even better.

He'd never had that reaction with anyone before, and while it scared him a little and made him feel like he wanted to back away, it also attracted him and made him want her to open her eyes and look at him some more.

"Madeline?"

Her eyes fluttered, then opened.

"Happy?" she asked, with that English accent and a touch of upper crust, and what else could he do but smile.

"I'll be happy when you're not bleeding anymore. Work on that."

"I would roll my eyes, but my head hurts."

"How bad does it hurt?" he asked, all humor fleeing and concern taking its place. She hadn't complained about pain before, had in fact downplayed the fact that her body even hurt. "Is your head the only place it hurts?"

"My butt hurts. But now that it's not sitting on the ground, it doesn't feel as bad as it did."

"I sure hope that's not your way of telling me that I need to look at it." He was teasing. Totally teasing. But after the words came out, he was afraid that maybe they'd come out wrong.

But she laughed. "No. I just realized I was lying. My butt doesn't hurt at all. There's no reason for anyone to need to look at it." She spoke fast, like she was concerned, but the little smile on her face belied the tone.

He grinned too. Okay, he hadn't thought he'd be joking with the classy English woman about looking at her butt. He wasn't quite sure what his mother would think about that anyway. He was old enough that it shouldn't matter, but she seemed to always be the litmus test in the back of his head about what was appropriate to do with women in particular and what wasn't. Some things a person just never outgrew. He might live by the Bible, but his mother was a very close second.

"I don't even want to know what you're thinking about." Madeline sighed and closed her eyes again.

THE BEAST GETS HIS COWGIRL IN THE SHOW ME STATE

"Thinking about my mother."

Her eyes popped open and scanned over his face. "You're serious."

"Sure am. Just figured she probably wouldn't think it was appropriate for me to be making butt jokes while I'm carrying a damsel in distress into my house." He walked over to the gate in the paddock and stopped in front of it. "Teddy," he called to the boy who was still unsaddling Missy. "Would you open this and let us through, please."

"Sure thing, Mr. Loyal."

"Is he here often?" Madeline asked without opening her eyes.

"Every day in the summer. I pay him a little to help me. He's a good help." He said that last line a little louder on purpose, because he wanted Teddy to hear. He suspected, although he didn't know for sure, that Teddy wasn't praised a lot at home. Actually, his home life probably wasn't much to speak of. His parents weren't completely neglectful, and they weren't abusive. They were just self-centered and uninterested in their children.

Their loss was his gain, because Teddy was a good kid and he loved having him around.

Teddy had the gate open. He walked through, careful not to hit Madeline's head on the post.

The gate clanked shut behind him. The chain rattled as Teddy hooked it.

He stopped and turned. "Once you have that tack put away, come on in. We'll have some hot chocolate together, or...you and I can drink hot chocolate, and Madeline can just lie on the couch and smell it."

"People are not going to be consuming hot chocolate in my presence without sharing it with me," Madeline murmured from his arms.

He looked down with a grin. "Yes, ma'am."

"Rad," Teddy said as he gave a wave and walked back to the horses. "Have they been fed yet today?" Teddy called over his shoulder.

"They have. And I watered them too, but you can top the trough off before you come in if you want. Don't let it overflow."

"I won't."

Madeline didn't weigh a lot, but she was getting heavy, and Loyal turned, striding toward the house.

"He seems like a nice kid. Eager to please."

"I think he's just happy for the attention. And yeah, he's a good kid. I trust him with the animals. I've watched him when he thinks I'm not around, and he treats them well. That's a mark of character."

"Who you are when no one is watching?" she asked, and maybe it was his imagination, but she seemed to snuggle closer to him. He liked it.

"Yeah." He thought of all the cameras that were on her, not constantly but often. "Who are you when the cameras are off?"

She huffed. One side of her lip tilted up, and one eye cracked. "You keep saying things that make me feel like you know things that maybe I don't want you to know."

It was just one eye, maybe half an eye, but it had the same power as both eyes full-on. That hypnotizing, looking into his soul, wanting to share all his secrets kind of power.

"Maybe I do."

They'd reached the porch. He went up the stairs. "This might get a little dicey; I need to open the door."

"You can put me down. I'm feeling a lot better. I think I would have been fine if I'd just waited for the dizzy spell to pass."

He thought the same thing, but he'd wanted to carry her. Wanted to hold her close, which was really strange, and he wasn't sure why he'd given in to the urge. Except he'd had an excuse as she struggled for balance.

He could have grabbed her arm. That was what he would have done normally—steadied her and let her get her feet under her before walking herself in.

There was something different about this woman.

But she had a face that was made to be in front of the camera, and he...didn't. Not to mention, this morning had shown him how different they were in other areas. He was a cowboy, a farmer, a rancher, all of that, and she, well, she couldn't even ride a horse.

If he were even going to consider marrying again, he needed a country girl. Lisa had taught him that lesson as well—someone who would be happy on the farm and not constantly needing attention in town.

Someone who could work with him, stay with him, ride with him.

Not that it had been anyone's fault the fighter jets had flown over, and he'd bet she'd get back on, even today if they had time. But the fact that she'd never been on a horse, never been on a farm, and had no clue about his life in any way put them in completely opposite life situations. Not really ones that were compatible.

"So is that accent for real?" Maybe it was a rude question, and he knew she was from the UK, but after living in America, surely she'd have lost it. Maybe it was part of her stage act. Although it hadn't slipped at all through everything. He assumed, unless it was really ingrained in her, she would have lost it when she got hurt.

"It's the one I was born with. The one I grew up speaking in the UK."

"You live in the US now?" he asked while his heart sank. He hadn't even considered until the words were on his tongue that she might only be in the US to record her show. He'd assumed she was here permanently.

If she lived in a completely different country, there was no way there could ever be anything between them, even if she wasn't a celebrity chef and he didn't have scars covering half his body.

Maybe that was true—it *was* true—but he didn't want to set her down. He shifted until he could reach the door handle while still holding her.

"I've been in the US for almost twelve years. It's funny you should mention my accent, because my UK friends say I'm losing it. Or at the very least that it's becoming Americanized."

Loyal hated to admit that her words made his heart jump. She didn't exactly say she was living in the US, but she had been here for twelve years and was losing her accent; maybe that meant she was serious about staying. Maybe he shouldn't push, but for some reason, it felt imperative to know.

"Are you staying in the US? Have you applied for citizenship?"

"My dad was a citizen. I have dual citizenship. For now, I'm staying, I guess. I have a house here, and friends. But my family is in the UK." Her voice had begun sounding more and more chipper, more like her old self. But now it kind of lowered, like she was ashamed. "I'm not a very good flyer." She huffed out a breath. "That's an understatement. I need a lot of drugs in order to be able to fly without completely panicking about being trapped inside the plane. So I don't go home often."

"So the United States is your home?" he pressed, still feeling, for some reason, like it was imperative to *know*.

"For now. Maybe when the celebrity chef thing ends," she paused, and he tensed, wondering if she were going to confess, but she kept going, "or when I retire, I might go back to the UK. There's nothing holding me here." It was the most thoughtful he'd heard her. She wasn't being flippant.

Maybe it was wrong of him, but he kind of hoped that something might start to hold her here.

Him.

Just as soon as that thought entered his head, he shoved it out of his mind, knowing it could never happen. He'd already given himself a lecture about her celebrity status and his scars.

God had taken that life away from him, the life where he might have been able to woo a celebrity chef and be equal with her.

A familiar surge of bitterness oozed through him like leakage from a toxic waste dump.

He wasn't going to put himself out there. Not again.

His ex-wife had lied to him, cheated on him, and never done what she said she was going to. It felt too raw and too risky to think about going through that again, scars or no scars.

He kicked the door shut with his foot after he walked through and strode toward the couch, ignoring her answer.

"I'm gonna set you down."

As soon as he started leaning forward, her arm tightened around his neck and she pressed closer to him. It felt good and right for her to hold him in this way, but again, those weren't feelings he welcomed.

Loyal continued to lean forward, setting her gently on the couch and only hesitating for a second, maybe two, before he slipped his arms out from underneath her. Her hand slid from his neck, leaving a coldness that had nothing to do with the temperature in the room and everything to do with the feeling around his heart.

He straightened.

"Thank you," she said softly, as though she were feeling the coldness too.

Wishful thinking on his part, he was sure.

"Dizzy?" he asked, standing beside the couch.

"No. I really think I'm going to be fine. Sore, of course, but fine. You're probably babying me more than you should."

"Better safe than sorry." His eyes roved over her. Her face was clear, although there were a few spots of blood on her temple, and her eyes were bright, and she seemed relaxed and mostly pain-free.

Still. "I'd feel better if you lie here for a bit while I make some hot chocolate. Teddy will be in soon."

"What's the story with him?" she asked, sincere concern in her eyes as she stared at him and waited for his answer.

"Same as with a million other kids. Home life isn't great, and he loves horses." He lifted his shoulder as he started to turn away. "So he comes here some evenings, weekends, and other days when there's no school. He spends a lot of time here in the summer. I like him."

All that was true from before the fire. Teddy had started to come around again in the time that Loyal had been back up and moving around himself. Maybe he'd been around while his brothers had been taking care of things; they hadn't really talked about it.

"He seems like a great kid. It's not easy to have someone extra hang around under your feet. I admire that. It says a lot about you." Her words were soft, and she almost looked at him with admiration, which made him uncomfortable.

He wasn't so sure about what she said anyway. Having Teddy around didn't make him someone to admire. It just meant he let a kid hang around, which was what any decent person would do, but he didn't argue and walked away.

Chapter 12

By the time he had the hot chocolate made and brought mugs into the living room, Madeline was sitting up with her feet flat on the floor. As he walked in, Teddy blew in the other door.

Madeline's eyes glanced up when they heard the door open, but she couldn't see he was coming in since Teddy used the side door.

"That's Teddy. He's just in time for a hot chocolate."

She smiled and nodded. "Does this mean I failed my first horseback riding lesson?"

"Anything less than death is success."

She pulled a face. "That's a low bar. I'm not sure how I feel about that."

"Maybe you should have asked for references before your entourage arrived." He handed her a hot chocolate, handle first.

"Noted for next time." She reached out, hooking her fingers in the handle. "Thank you. It smells delicious." She tilted her head and gave him what he would have said was a flirtatious glance, only it couldn't have been. "Did you make it from scratch?"

"Are you asking if I milked the cow?" He pursed his lips and blew on the hot liquid. "No."

She chuckled as he'd intended. "I didn't ask if you were God and created milk out in the kitchen. I only wanted to know if you made the chocolate from scratch."

He held both hands out in innocence, but the effect was slightly ruined because he was holding a chocolate mug in one hand. "The chocolate is totally and completely from the store. Maybe you won't drink it now?"

She wasn't a snob that way. He hadn't been around her enough to actually witness it, but he knew instinctively that wasn't the kind of person she was.

She gave one of those upper-crust sniffs she was so good at and arched one brow at him. "Of course not. Artificial colors. Artificial flavors. Sugar." She gave an exaggerated shiver. "All that offends my delicate sensibilities. There's no way I could ever allow this travesty to touch my lips." She lifted the mug and took a sip. "This is lovely. Thank you."

He laughed at her goofing off, glad that her natural exuberance and funny personality was coming back.

Teddy walked in on stocking feet. He'd been in the house enough to watch Loyal, and although Loyal hadn't stopped today to take his boots off since he'd been carrying Madeline, he almost always did, and Teddy did too. It reminded Loyal of the saying "more is caught than taught," because he'd never specifically told Teddy he needed to take his shoes off when he came inside.

He lifted the hot chocolate he'd set on the coffee table and said to Teddy, "This is yours. And there's more where that came from. We might have to give Miss Madeline a break, but I can make breakfast for us. Or I guess it's more like brunch." He didn't bother to ask Teddy if he was hungry. He knew what that answer would be.

"Give Miss Madeline a break?" Teddy asked, taking a long swig of his hot chocolate. "What do you mean by that?"

"Because of her being a chef. I think she might be a little too beat-up to cook for us this morning, so I figured you and I would do it for her."

Teddy's eyes lit up, and Loyal's lips turned up in a small smile.

He'd been careful to place himself so that his good side was toward Madeline, so he didn't flinch when she looked at him with a smile of her own.

He hadn't taken Teddy under his wing to get brownie points from anyone. He'd done it because it had seemed like the right thing to do

THE BEAST GETS HIS COWGIRL IN THE SHOW ME STATE 109

when Teddy had started hanging around, petting the horses, and asking questions. But he could admit that he liked the way Madeline was looking at him, and he liked that she knew that he was more than just a cowboy with a bunch of scars. It gave him the same feeling in his chest that walking into the barn and smelling all those familiar and well-loved smells gave him—a comforting peace to his soul.

He and Teddy worked in the kitchen, not making anything fancy, just some vegetable omelets. It didn't take long, but long enough for Madeline to get up off the couch and walk into the kitchen as he was flipping the omelet for the last time.

He looked up, scanning over her immediately and a little concerned.

"No dizziness?" he asked. He wanted to tell her she shouldn't be up, shouldn't be out, but he had hated it when people told him that when he was recuperating from his burns. Being up felt like an accomplishment, and it irked him when people diminished that.

"No. I could smell your omelets all the way from the couch. Plus," she held up her empty mug, "I'm out of hot chocolate."

"Man. That's too bad. I haven't had time to go milk the cow. The black one that gives chocolate milk."

Teddy laughed from where he was wiping the counter.

"That's not funny," Madeline said. "I grew up, not exactly in the city, but definitely not on a farm or even in the country, and used to believe that. It does make sense." She said the last line defensively in a goofy way that had Loyal's lips turning up.

He had lost count of how many times that had happened this morning.

He couldn't deny that Madeline had made him feel at ease more than anyone else ever had.

He hadn't even remembered to turn his head and hide his scars.

They were just setting their plates on the bar when the doorbell interrupted them.

At first, mild curiosity was all that stirred inside of him when he heard it. But then his chest tightened and his neck clinched, and he almost dropped the plate of eggs he was setting down as his fingers wanted to spasm.

Lisa was supposed to arrive this afternoon, and it could be her. Early, but that wouldn't surprise him. She liked to keep him caught off guard, and she might've said afternoon when she really meant eleven o'clock.

Madeline's eyes were on him, and she probably saw all the emotions that ran across his face. "Your ex?"

He lifted his shoulder. "Only one way to find out."

"We never decided how we're going to play this." He wouldn't say there was panic in her voice, but she definitely had lost any goofy tones.

"You're right, but I don't know what to say." His hands were sweating. Patty would be with her if this was his ex.

He longed with his whole soul to have a relationship with his daughter. She'd been five when the fire happened. It had been two years since he felt her arms around his neck or heard her call him Daddy.

His ex had tried once before Christmas to drop her off, but Patty would have nothing to do with him, and Lisa hadn't allowed her to stay. Before that, it had been summer. Before that, he'd been too laid up to hope to have Patty do more than visit, which Lisa had not allowed her to do—bad memories.

"I'll follow your lead wherever it goes," Madeline said softly, standing from the stool she'd been sitting on but staying beside the bar, as though waiting for him to tell her whether he wanted her to follow him out the door or wait in the kitchen.

Her words surprised him. He knew she'd agreed to help, but he hadn't expected blind loyalty—following his lead wherever. He'd thought they'd work something out and stick to a script.

Too late for that now.

THE BEAST GETS HIS COWGIRL IN THE SHOW ME STATE

After everything he'd been through, feeling grateful wasn't a new situation for him. But still, it was humbling to show gratitude, and he looked down at the floor before lifting his head. "Thank you. I appreciate that."

She nodded, her eyes serious, as he turned and walked out of the kitchen and through the dining room. It didn't take long before he could see the door and the tall slim figure of Lisa. She'd always cropped her hair short, and he'd always thought it made her look cute, especially considering how tall she was. Tall and slender.

There was no denying she was a beautiful woman. She'd always been nice, too. Even when she wasn't allowing his daughter to stay with him, she had done it in a nice way.

They'd never fought. Not much anyway. Never her. It was always his temper. He supposed a man had a right to a temper when he found out his wife had been cheating and lying to him.

He'd always hated liars and never understood them. Particularly compulsive liars. Why was it so hard to speak the truth?

He was judging and being harsh, probably because of the bitterness he held toward Lisa. Telling the truth was a hard thing, lying was easy, and he knew it. Still, being lied to sucked. He would rather she took a stick and beat him with it than lie to him.

But he hadn't gotten to choose the pain she inflicted.

He only got to choose his response.

He hated the thought that popped into his head, although he knew it was true. So far, he'd been choosing the wrong response, allowing Lisa to cause turmoil in his chest and life and screw up his brain, making him an angry, bitter man.

Lisa might have been the one doing the lying, but God was the one who had allowed it into his life.

For Loyal to get angry and blame Lisa and be mad at her, and hate all liars, and tell himself he hated all liars was just him saying God didn't know what He was doing when He allowed Lisa to lie and cheat.

God could have stopped it.

Instead of being comforting, that line made him bitter too.

Because, yeah, God could have stopped it. God could have kept his family together. God could have kept his wife home and true.

But he hadn't.

Loyal still hadn't figured out why. Somehow, just the fact that God was God, the Creator of the universe, and Master of everything, the One who gave him life and sustained him, didn't seem to negate Loyal's desire and need to know why.

Which was a lack of faith.

Faith would believe without seeing that whatever God allowed into his life was right.

A lack of faith needed proof.

Loyal put his hand on the doorknob and pulled it open.

"Loyal, darling." His ex-wife stepped forward and gave him a small air hug, brushing his cheek. She'd always been affectionate, and he tried to at least be decent to her, for Patty's sake.

He allowed the hugging and the kiss, although he didn't return either.

His eyes were drawn instead to the little girl who stared at him with wide, frightened eyes and tried to hide behind her mother. His heart broke a little, as it did every time he saw Patty do that.

"Hello, sweetie," he said softly.

Lisa froze, and it felt like her mask slipped a little before she composed herself and stepped back.

"Come on, Patty darling, let's go in. Mommy won't leave you."

It did grate on his nerves the way Lisa acted like Patty was right to be terrified of him. He had wondered some if Lisa had pushed Patty, either intentionally or unintentionally, toward being even more scared of him.

But it was a passing thought, and he had absolutely no proof to back it up, so he pushed it out of his head. His mom had offered to watch Patty and talk to her about Loyal and how he'd saved her life. Good things, just in case Lisa was at home making him sound like the devil or worse.

But when Patty wouldn't calm down around Loyal, Lisa wouldn't let her stay with Loyal's mom.

Wanting to keep the peace, Loyal had never thought about pushing harder. It probably wouldn't have done any good anyway. Now that he was feeling better, and knowing this was the way he was going to look for the rest of his life, he was willing to battle a little more to try to push for what he wanted.

They'd stepped in and shut the door behind them, and he'd stepped back to give them room. As he stood there, his eyes were drawn toward the doorway to the hall and dining room. Madeline stood there, waiting.

Chapter 13

Maybe Madeline should have sat in the kitchen until he needed her, but she couldn't. She wasn't sure just when things had shifted for her, from Loyal being someone she had to put up with to someone she cared about, but it had happened.

Maybe it was his gentleness and taking care of her after she'd fallen, or maybe it was the sense of humor that she wouldn't have guessed he had, or maybe it was the way his smile seemed rusty and indicated a lot of suffering.

She suspected it was all of those and something else. Something she couldn't name but that pulled her toward him and had from the first. Whether it was attraction, or whether it was something else. Something deeper.

She assumed the tall woman standing just inside the door was Loyal's ex. She was beautiful. Tall and slender and poised.

Everything that Madeline should be but wasn't.

Her goofy and quirky personality was what made the show successful and what had given her the ability to hide her inability to cook. But that didn't mean that she didn't long to have the natural grace and composure that the woman standing in front of her had.

Obviously, Loyal was attracted to women like that. Who wouldn't be?

Well, she would never be poised, and she would never be tall, and she would never have that classic beauty. But she could keep her word. And she could be true. She'd given both her loyalty and her word to Loyal, and she intended to follow through.

So she left her post at the door and walked over to Loyal, stopping beside him and putting her fingers gently on his upper arm.

THE BEAST GETS HIS COWGIRL IN THE SHOW ME STATE

The touch was a mistake. She already knew the solid feel of his body and the way it affected hers, but she hadn't realized it would be such a distraction as fissures of awareness spread through her fingers while her brain registered the solid muscle of his biceps.

The woman's brows went up at Madeline's familiar gesture toward Loyal.

Madeline wasn't sure how Loyal felt about her bold move, but he didn't move away, so she didn't either.

"Looks like someone's been busy." Lisa spoke, not unkindly but with a little frost in her tone. Her eyes narrowed as she zeroed in on Madeline. "You look familiar. Are you from around here?"

Madeline smiled; all she had to do was speak, and the woman would know that she was most definitely not from Missouri.

Before she could say anything, Loyal said, "Lisa, this is my very good friend Madeline. Madeline, this is my ex-wife, Lisa. Behind her is my daughter, Patty." His voice softened as he introduced his daughter, and there was no mistaking the love in his tone.

It made Madeline's heart ache to hear it. To know the pain that he felt for not being able to see her and not having her be able to stand to be around him.

Well, she might be able to do something about that. Children had always loved her. She could make her quirky and goofy personality twist just a little, and it went from being humor that adults loved to a sparkle that drew children.

She had her triplet sisters to thank for that, and a mum who worked all the time and left a lot of the babysitting duties to the older sister.

Maybe part of her draw toward Loyal and part of the heartache she felt was knowing that she had grown up without a dad because her dad wasn't interested.

Patty had the opportunity to grow up with a dad—a dad who loved her and longed for her—which was something Madeline had always wished for. Madeline might be able to heal a little girl's heartache and also help a dad whose heart was breaking as well.

How could she not give this her best shot?

She squeezed Loyal's arm before stepping forward, her hand outstretched. "It's very nice to meet you, Lisa. And no, I'm not from around here. But I am staying here for a bit." She gave a smile that was friendly and warm, and met Lisa's eyes as they shook. "Your daughter is adorable. She has her father's amazing eyes and your exquisite bone structure."

The compliment, sincere, made Lisa relax. Madeline didn't believe in saying something she didn't mean. Although she might not be enamored with Lisa's personality, there was no question as to whether or not she was beautiful. Patty truly did have her bone structure.

"Thank you so much." Lisa gave a small smile as she looked down and slightly behind her at her daughter.

Madeline didn't doubt that she loved her. She could see it in her eyes. But she also thought that Lisa probably could have done more to help her daughter love her father and want to spend time with him. That was a big judgment, but something in the standoffish way Lisa had toward Loyal made Madeline feel like there might be a competition there or something to prove.

Madeline supposed she could ask Loyal, but she doubted he'd tell her, even if he did know what was up with Lisa. Women could be complicated.

Lisa's hand tapped her daughter's head. "I'm sure you know about the fire. It left scars on Patty as well. Thankfully not her face. But it also scarred her psyche. Her psychiatrist says that eventually she'll probably work through it but that we shouldn't rush her or force her to stay with him when it brings back painful memories. She did lose a brother in the fire. Not to mention she's had horrible nightmares. She associates Loyal with all that."

Lisa's voice was appropriately soft, and she spoke like she was confiding something.

Madeline wasn't sure whether Patty could hear her or not, or even truly understand what her mother was saying. Maybe.

Regardless, Madeline nodded sympathetically. "Oh, how awful."

Then, she put on her kid smile and peeked behind Lisa, feeling a little like a kid herself, and not liking that feeling next to Lisa's poise, but shoving that discomfort aside. She was doing this for Loyal. And Patty.

"Hey there, sweetheart. I'm Madeline, like the book." She quoted a few lines from the book, and Patty's eyes perked up, although she stayed behind her mother's leg.

Madeline knelt to the floor, not allowing her face to wince as her head wound twitched and pain shot across her skull. She just hoped it didn't start bleeding. That would be very inopportune.

She pulled out the bit of paper and the pen that she'd stuck in her pocket earlier before she walked out of the kitchen and decided that her dignity needed to be sacrificed.

She plopped down on her butt on the floor. "Sometimes, when we can't talk, a picture works better." She put the paper down on the floor where Patty could see it clearly and then drew a cartoonish picture of a horse. Making it cute, to appeal to her little-girl side, but also a little bit goofy, to appeal to the child in her.

Beside her, Patty shifted impatiently, but a little further away out of her peripheral vision, Loyal had stilled, almost frozen in place, as he watched her.

She knew, technically, that God never got tired of hearing from her, from his people, but sometimes she thought she bugged Him more than normal folks did. Still, she sent up a quick prayer.

Lord, Loyal's been through a lot, would You let him have his daughter back? Please. Let this work.

She started talking as she drew. "I was riding a horse this morning. She was really pretty. And I think she liked me." She looked up under her lashes and gave a little smile, because even a child likes to think that other people and things like them.

As she suspected, Patty's lips pulled back at that. A shy smile, one that reminded her so much of Loyal that Madeline had to remind herself to not stare.

She looked back at the paper. "My horse was graceful and sweet, and I liked her a lot too. But," she said as she made the mane and tail long and flowing and beautiful on the paper, "I was scared, because I've never ridden a horse before."

After she said this, she looked up again, knowing that Patty could commiserate about being scared as well. Sure enough, Patty looked at her solemnly, with several emotions tracking across her facial features: fear, wonder, and confusion that this adult was sitting on the floor and chatting about horses liking her and being scared. It probably was not the type of behavior she was used to expecting out of adults.

Madeline had never been accused of acting with the expected behaviors.

The opposite most of the time.

"I was way up high on her back, and she moved when I wasn't expecting her to, but your daddy held her, and he talked softly to her, and she settled down, and so did I. Your daddy helped me not be afraid."

She finished the drawing of the horse and turned it so that it was facing right-side up for Patty.

Patty looked at the drawing, studying it for a moment before she whispered, "Pretty."

Madeline wasn't sure whether she should go on or not.

She decided to go for it.

She turned the paper back to her and started drawing herself, not on the horse but falling off.

She started talking again in that same matter-of-fact voice. "We weren't expecting it, and neither was my horse, but some really loud airplanes went over and scared her. She moved when I wasn't expecting it, and neither was your daddy, and since I'm not very good at riding horses, I fell off."

She didn't pause here, because she wanted to make sure that Patty kept listening. "It hurt, but your daddy was able to calm the horse, and he carried me inside and made sure that I was okay too." She drew a really goofy expression on her face as she fell off the horse in the picture, one that she was sure would make Patty laugh and not be scared.

"Sometimes bad things happen, but I trusted your daddy, and he took care of me." She turned the paper around again. She'd also drawn Loyal standing beside her, catching her. That wasn't exactly the way it happened, but it wasn't like she was lying. She'd never said that the picture was what happened.

Plus, she liked the way the drawing showed what happened better.

"Your dad is pretty special," she said. Patty looked at the drawing. Madeline kept her eyes on her and met her serious gaze as Patty looked up from the picture.

"I want to draw horses too." Patty's voice was soft and a little hesitant.

Madeline smiled reassuringly and held up the pen. "I'll share. Do you want to draw on this side of the paper, or do you want to draw on the other side?"

Patty came slowly out from behind her mum and sat gingerly down on the floor beside Madeline, taking the pen and paper.

Madeline talked to Patty, and eventually Loyal's voice rumbled above her, in low tones, and Lisa's voice came, with tones of annoyance, answering.

Madeline didn't mean to eavesdrop, and she really didn't, not completely, since her entire focus was on Patty and getting her to trust her and developing a rapport with her.

Her goal was to move from drawing horses to wanting to go pet them.

Loyal had mentioned the night that they talked that he and Patty had had horses and the kitchen in common. Madeline assumed Patty still loved horses.

Madeline didn't want to rush it, though. Kids could be very slow to warm up, and Patty had some very real issues.

So while Loyal and Lisa argued softly but intensely about the custody arrangement, and whether they should get a lawyer involved or not, Madeline focused on Patty, catching occasional snatches of the conversation without really trying.

At one time, Teddy must have come out, because Lisa's voice raised some, and she said quite clearly, "Is that little ragamuffin still hanging around here? And in the house! You don't know when the last time was that he had a bath."

Madeline cringed because she was sure Teddy heard.

"It's my house. He's a great kid. I like him. He helps me, and he's also a good friend."

Madeline's hackles lowered. Loyal had done a good job of defending him.

Teddy must have gone back in the kitchen, because nothing more was said, and when Madeline got a chance to look around, she didn't see him.

Lisa had moved away from Patty when she and Loyal started talking, and Patty hadn't even noticed. Their voices had faded to low murmurs when, after about thirty minutes and four pages of pictures, Patty had started chattering, almost to the point of Madeline not being able to get a word in edgewise, about horses and ponies and manes and tails and how she used to ride and how she had horses in her room and horses on her blanket and horses on her ceiling and how her birthday cake had horses on it. That was when Madeline decided she could take a risk.

"It's fun to draw pictures of horses and have horses all around us on all our stuff, but maybe you'd like to go out and actually pet the horses?" Madeline smiled her most engaging kids' smile, and by that time, Patty was smiling back with no problem.

Patty didn't even hesitate. "Yes! I want to go pet the horses. I want to ride horses." She dropped her pencil and jumped up, looking at Madeline expectantly.

Horses were definitely not something that Madeline was any good at, and the thumping in her head was a constant reminder of that fact. But hey, she was a world-famous chef and she couldn't cook, so why not?

"Ask your mommy if you can go out. If she says yes, we'll go pet some horses."

"I want to ride." Patty's face was still happy, but her brows had drawn down a little. It was a demand.

"I'm just learning to ride, so I know I can't help you with that. But if your mommy will let you go out, maybe your daddy will help you ride."

At the mention of her daddy, the pout disappeared from her face and a little bit of fear crossed it, just a shade, but it colored it to the point that Madeline took a step and closed the gap between them, holding her hand out.

Patty put her hand in hers and smiled up. She said softly, "If you ask Mommy, she might say yes."

Madeline had to smile at that. She'd been an only child for a long time before her triplet sisters were born, but that didn't mean she hadn't tried to work her mother the exact same way.

"I sure can." She was thrilled that Patty was willing to go, her hand resting comfortably and trustingly in hers. She felt the weight of responsibility, a tightening in her chest that signaled nervousness, but overshadowing all of that were zaps of excitement. Maybe this would really work out.

She looked over at Lisa and opened her mouth, but Lisa was already shaking her head. "No. Patty's been through so much. I don't want her to risk injury by going out to the horses."

And maybe it wouldn't work out.

Beyond Lisa, Loyal's face darkened, and Madeline opened her mouth before he could, because she didn't want any angry words, no matter how softly uttered, to scare Patty and the fragile trust that Patty was giving them.

Not that she thought Loyal was an angry man or that he was going to yell. It was just that Patty seemed to be doing okay, and Madeline didn't want to risk having that go backwards.

"Do you think Patty's psychiatrist would say that it would be good for her to go out and pet the horses if she wants to?" Madeline eased the sting of her words with a sweet smile, all the while knowing that she was basically telling Lisa that the psychiatrist would say that if Patty was okay going out with the horses, it would be really good for her to have this link to her former life.

She had faults and hang-ups, of course, but Lisa truly did care about her child and helping her get over the trauma that she went through. Still, if there weren't issues there, she would not be saying no but rather would be all on board with petting the horses.

Lisa knew she'd been outmaneuvered. Her lips flattened, and the tone of friendliness that had been on her face faded as her eyes narrowed, and she looked at Madeline with renewed interest and suspicion.

She sighed, a put-out sound. "If you have to, I suppose you're right. But I don't want to go out to the barn." A superior smile curved her lips up as her eyes flicked to her daughter. "Mommy's not going out, so you have to go out with the lady." Her tone lowered, sounding almost ominous. "And your daddy."

The tone she used made Madeline's fingers curl, and she had to focus to straighten them.

That woman was deliberately trying to scare her daughter away from her dad. Madeline's teeth ground together around her happy smile. It wasn't very often that she wanted to grab someone by the hair and body slam them to the floor, but the image of Lisa pile-driving into the hardwood was sweetly satisfying.

"We can trust your daddy to take care of us. Remember the picture?" Madeline said in her sweetest and most child-friendly voice, using her most beguiling smile and meeting the eyes that looked up at her so trustingly.

Patty nodded, but she sucked an upper lip, too, and her eyes were unsure.

In Madeline's experience, it was always better to give kids a little room, so as much as it was counterintuitive for her, she backed off. "We don't have to if you don't want to. I'm sure there will be plenty of other opportunities to pet the horses. The horses out there are very pretty."

Sometimes sentences didn't have to go together in order to make sense to a child. She kinda threw that last sentence in there. It had nothing to do with anything, except Madeline was reminding her about how much she loved horses, even though she was being given the opportunity to back out.

"I want to go pet them. I want to pet the pretty one that you rode today. The one that we drew."

"I want to pet her too. I want to thank her for listening to your daddy and calming down."

Patty smiled, and Madeline returned it.

Chapter 14

Loyal stood with the lead rope in his hand, holding Missy while Patty and Madeline petted her.

He could barely take his eyes off his little girl. It was thrilling to actually be standing near her, sharing his love of horses with her. He knew she still loved them, and it could be a link that connected them, along with the kitchen and cooking. Just like they had before the fire.

It wasn't that he didn't want Lisa involved at all. Lisa was her mom, and Patty would want to know her as well, but he hated being shut out the way he'd been the last two years.

This was the first time he'd been with Patty away from Lisa since the fire.

He had Madeline to thank for that.

Okay, maybe it was easier than he'd thought to take his eyes off Patty, because he didn't mind resting them on Madeline.

Sweet and alive, she practically glowed with happiness and kindness. Patty had only known her for an hour or so, and yet she hung on Madeline's every word and looked at her with adoring eyes.

Which was fine by Loyal. If Patty adored Madeline, there was every chance that she would allow Lisa to walk away and she would stay here.

"This horse likes me," Patty said as she scratched Missy's nose.

"She really does. Look at her putting her head down so you can reach it. I think she thinks you scratch her nose better than anybody." Madeline's voice held a cute note that seemed to really appeal to Patty.

Patty grinned, a pleased-with-herself smile.

Loyal shifted, thrilled that Patty was once again enjoying what they had loved to do together before the fire.

THE BEAST GETS HIS COWGIRL IN THE SHOW ME STATE

Maybe it was his movement that caught her eye, but Patty's gaze shifted over to him. Some of the joy faded from her face, and a little bit of wariness crept in, but she blinked and said, "You can pet her too."

Loyal's heart couldn't get any more full. She was inviting him to come over and be a part of what they were doing. He certainly wasn't going to turn that down.

He stepped over and ran a hand down the broad back. He wouldn't saddle Missy again, not today, but he did ask, "Would you like to sit on her back?"

Cognizant that he needed to be more alert than he had been earlier that day when the fighter jets had scared Madeline's horse, and also realizing he'd never apologized for that, Loyal almost held his breath while he waited for Patty's answer.

It wasn't long in coming. She nodded eagerly, her eyes glowing and her cheeks rosy.

"I'm going to keep the lead rope in one hand, and I'm going to pick you up with the other and throw you over. Just the way we used to do it." He had to add that last bit in because Patty and he had had a lot of fun together, and he wanted her to remember that. They were beautiful memories for him. He hoped she had some of the same, that the fire hadn't ruined everything.

Her face didn't cloud, and he considered it a win as she turned and allowed him to put his arm around her and lift her onto the horse. It was like his scars weren't even there.

And he was very aware that it was Madeline who had made everyone forget.

Not everyone.

Patty.

He settled Patty on the horse and kept his arm behind her, but as soon as she was settled, he couldn't keep his eyes from going to Madeline. The gratefulness in his heart, and the appreciation for what she'd done for him, even if Patty didn't stay, just to be able to spend a few minutes with the horses he loved and the daughter he adored, was worth more than all the money in the world.

She lifted her eyes, feeling his on hers probably, and raised her brows in question, her eyes searching his.

He shifted a little away from Patty, keeping his hand on the horse just to be safe, and said, soft and low, "Thank you. Thank you so much."

There was more in his heart he wanted to say. For the first time in years, he had feelings—good feelings—he wanted to express, and they were so close to tumbling out of his mouth.

But he pressed his lips together. He could tell her how beautiful he thought she was. How alive and sweet and kind and perfect. How she made him feel things that he never thought he'd feel again, deeper things he'd never felt before. How he could look at her and get excited about life again.

And even more, how he could picture them together. How his fingers itched to trace the softness of her cheek. How he didn't feel like he was close enough. How his arms ached to go around her and pull her to him. How he breathed deep, just to catch a whiff of her scent, and how that scent swirled and touched every good thing inside of him and made him warm and happy, and he could almost believe he was whole again.

No, he definitely didn't want to go there. Because, not only was it way too soon—they barely knew each other—but nothing between them could ever work out.

He did owe her, however, and he just might be able to help her.

MADELINE COULDN'T BELIEVE that Lisa had left Patty with them. But she had.

THE BEAST GETS HIS COWGIRL IN THE SHOW ME STATE

Lisa had waited for an hour or more inside the house before coming out to the horses and telling them that she was leaving. Patty hadn't seemed to care.

She hadn't clung to her father but instead had gripped Madeline. It was still progress. She'd been fine holding Madeline as Lisa drove away. Comfortable with the horses, having a great time.

They had spent the afternoon there, with Teddy as well, who came around after Lisa had left and stayed when they went in and cooked supper.

Thankfully, Madeline's head had allowed her to sit on a barstool and watch, without too many questions being asked. Patty seemed happy helping Loyal and Teddy, and the chicken casserole that they'd made had been simple yet amazingly delicious. If Madeline had been in any doubt that the kitchen was for show, supper had removed it.

When they had finished eating, Teddy went home, and they'd spent a little time playing some games. When Loyal's phone rang, he'd whispered that it was Lisa, and Madeline had taken Patty upstairs to let her take a shower while he talked.

In her experience with children, bedtime was always a little touchy, and if there was going to be any homesickness at all, it would be then. Lisa probably knew that, and although Madeline hated to assume that she timed her call for that purpose, the idea was there. Whether or not she had though, Madeline would do her best to distract Patty.

"Things are taken care of. I appreciate it." Loyal's voice startled her as she stood in the hall, looking out of the window, listening to the shower running.

"No problem." She would do that and a lot more for him. She'd do it for anyone, but there was something about Loyal, and even now just looking at him, she got that fire in the pit of her stomach that crackled out and made her fingertips burn.

She didn't know what it was about him, but she couldn't look at him or be around him without feeling it.

He held up Patty's jammies. "I'll put these on the bed in the spare room."

His eyes seemed shadowed, and so much of the carefree, easygoing spirit that he'd had most of the day had been wiped away.

The shower shut off. Madeline looked at the door before she said, "I'll make sure she knows that when she gets out."

It wasn't her place to say anything, but she hated the tightness in his face and the loss of his smile. "Was your phone call that bad?"

Chapter 15

Loyal had started to turn away, but his eyes snapped back to hers, searching, as though trying to figure out how she knew his phone call had gone badly. His lips tightened.

"She wanted to come get Patty. It's frustrating." He shoved a hand through his hair before letting it slip down the side. "I haven't seen her for two years, and Lisa's acting like me having her for an afternoon and overnight is too much."

Madeline wasn't sure what to say about that. Lisa was definitely in the wrong here, but Loyal already knew that.

"She's going to let her stay?" She could assume that because he'd unpacked the jammies.

"Yes. But I don't know for how long. Usually when she comes in to see her folks, it's for a week." He shoved his hand in his pocket. "If I have to fight just to have her for a day, I'm probably gonna have to go to court in order to get to see her for any length of time. There's been so much struggle, so much fight. It would be nice to just have her work with me. Surely she wants her daughter to know her dad too. I don't understand…" His voice trailed off, like maybe he did know why Lisa was giving him such a hard time.

Madeline waited, but he didn't say anything else, and she wasn't sure what to ask to get him to open up about it. Or even if she should. Although she wanted to.

He seemed to take a moment and gather himself, then he turned to her fully. "I appreciate what you did today. My mom tried to help, and I know that she still would, but no one's been able to do what you did—to win her trust so quickly, which is what had to happen with the way Lisa keeps her away. I appreciate that, and I'd like to do something in return."

His eyes darkened a little, and he took a step forward. She didn't think he was thinking he wanted to kiss her in return for what she'd done, but the air seemed to crackle between them, and her heart shivered.

It wasn't a kiss in exchange. It was almost like he got distracted by his desire, if she wasn't misreading the emotion in his eyes.

She hoped she wasn't.

Even though nothing could come of it, and he probably didn't feel anything more than the same attraction that tugged at her, she still wanted it.

Even knowing that because of the deeper feelings that had been growing in her towards him, it could end up being painful for her, she didn't back away.

His eyes held hers as he stopped with just a few inches separating them, his eyes dark and hooded and deep.

Anticipation swirled, and she leaned forward, not quite brave enough to take that last step, to close the distance between them, to meet him halfway.

He shook his head. Like coming out of a trance. His eyes opened and cleared, and he leaned back. His voice still held a note of fuzziness as he asked, "Is there anything that I can do for you?"

Almost the way he said it, or maybe it was the tilt of his head as he studied her, but she thought he was referring to the fact that she couldn't cook. Where she got that idea, she couldn't say. Maybe it was just her own guilt that always brought that deception to her forefront.

She would prefer a kiss.

Although, when it came time that they were doing the live show, she might have preferred his help there.

Could she trust him?

THE BEAST GETS HIS COWGIRL IN THE SHOW ME STATE

She felt like she threw herself out—loving liberally, giving kindness without reservation, and trusting liberally—all except in this.

"Anything at all?" he prodded.

She could tell him. She could trust him. The feeling was deep and settled in her soul. She was sure of it.

"Maybe there is." She took a breath, but before she could say anything, the bathroom door opened, and Patty stood there wrapped in a towel.

"I don't have any clothes."

Loyal held out the jammies he had unpacked. "Your mom left these for you. I can show you where your room is, and you can get dressed, okay?"

Her little chin went up and down, but a warning signal shot through Madeline's brain. It almost looked like her lip was getting ready to tremble, and her eyes didn't hold the confidence that they had had all day while they'd been petting the horses and working in the kitchen and playing games.

She was feeling homesick for all things familiar, including her mother.

Loyal showed Patty which room and then allowed her to go in and close the door behind her.

Madeline followed him down the hall and stopped in front of him. "I think you might need to distract her a little before bedtime. The look in her eyes... I think she's going to want her mother. Maybe we can tell her a story?"

She was way taking liberties. Patty was Loyal's. But he seemed willing to share, and Patty hadn't actually gone to him yet. Though from what Madeline could see, it was just a matter of time.

Patty definitely had had a bond with him before the fire. Madeline could see that, because Patty almost instinctively trusted him. Unfortunately, whatever had happened the night of fire, combined with what seemed like a total lack of any effort on Lisa's part to try to help her get over it in regards to Loyal, had hurt her trust.

"There are some books in her room. But I used to sing to her before..." Loyal looked away, like thinking about his life before the fire was somehow painful, or maybe it was just the fact that he didn't want to recreate that.

Madeline had a feeling that was it. "You don't have to do everything the same as you did before the fire, but you could use that to build, like you're doing with the horses and the kitchen. Similar, but different. New. But familiar."

She hoped she was on the right track.

Her shoulders relaxed as Loyal nodded. Thoughtful. Like maybe he was thinking about more than just Patty.

It was the same with his face and the scars and the life he had to build after that. The same, but different. Familiar, yet new. He had to let go.

And trust.

He shifted, and she breathed in; already his scent was familiar and welcome, settling in her soul like a soft, warm blanket.

That look was back in his eye, and her heart had the same response. Wanting her to go closer, not wanting to miss another opportunity.

His hand came up, and her eyes fluttered as his fingers stroked gently down her hair and just brushed her neck, landing on her shoulder.

"Madeline, I—"

The door opened, his hand dropped, and she jerked her head. Patty stood there, blinking at them. "I want my mom."

Madeline's eyes met Loyal's. She wanted to close her eyes and groan.

But she put on a bright smile and walked forward, taking both of Patty's hands in hers and lifting her arms up. "I love the horses on your jammies. They're so pretty. Just like the ones that we were petting today."

Patty smiled. "My sheets have horses on them too. So does my blanket. Do you want to see?"

Madeline's eyes slid closed before she allowed Patty to pull her into her room.

They looked at her blankets and admired them before Madeline said, "Can we snuggle under your horse blanket for a bit? Your dad said he would sing to us."

Patty's eyes went to Loyal. Remembrance flickered across her face, like this was a familiar thing, just forgotten, until now.

Her hand squeezed Madeline's, and she climbed into bed and slid over. Madeline slid in beside her, and they pulled the covers up.

Loyal stood at the foot of the bed, as though unsure where he should go. Madeline's heart cracked for him. It hurt to see him and the obvious love he had for his daughter and know that he was risking rejection and heartache by putting himself out like he had been.

"Is it okay if I come around and sit down on the other side of you?" he asked softly, looking at Patty.

Madeline bit her lips, because she wanted so badly for Patty to say yes, for her to ease the insecurity and uncertainty from his face and cause him to smile. But she couldn't make Patty give the right answer to his question, so she kept her mouth closed and just prayed that God would move Patty to say yes.

God did one better. Patty added a "please" to her "yes."

Relief made her weak, and she slumped, catching Loyal's eyes as he walked around the bed. It was thoughtful, like he'd seen how much she was pulling for him and he appreciated it.

He sat down on the bed, his back against the headboard and his stocking feet stretched out. Madeline couldn't stop her smile as Patty shifted over and laid her head on the pillow beside him. His hand came down and stroked her hair in a fatherly and familiar way, and Patty smiled.

"What do you want me to sing?"

Patty's shoulders lifted in a shrug. Loyal didn't ask again. He just started.

> *When He cometh, when He cometh,*
> *To make up His jewels,*
> *All His jewels, precious jewels,*
> *His loved and His own.*

It was a hymn that was familiar to her from her childhood. An easy tune, simple and sweet, and from the look on Patty's face, she would guess it was one of her favorites. Her little body snuggled closer to her dad, and his hand, big and rough and scarred, cupped her shoulder.

When Madeline joined him on the chorus, he sang the harmony, and Patty hummed along.

Like the stars of the morning,
His bright crown adorning,
They shall shine in their beauty,
Bright gems for His crown.

Madeline let Loyal sing the second verse by himself. She wasn't sure of the words.

> *He will gather, He will gather*
> *The gems for His kingdom,*
> *All the pure ones, all the bright ones,*
> *His loved and His own.*

She came in easily on the chorus again, and again he sang the harmony almost immediately.

Patty still hummed, but maybe softer.

Like the stars of the morning,
His bright crown adorning,
They shall shine in their beauty,
Bright gems for His crown.

It'd been a big day, she'd been on an airplane before she'd even arrived at their house, and her body relaxed under the gentle music as Loyal started the third verse and Madeline sang the harmony on the chorus.

Little children, little children,
Who love their Redeemer,
Are the jewels, precious jewels,
His loved and His own.
Like the stars of the morning,
His bright crown adorning,
They shall shine in their beauty,
Bright gems for His crown.

Their voices blended and held on the last note before fading off into the darkness and becoming memories—sweet, happy memories that wrapped around them like a ribbon on a Christmas gift, enclosing them in their own special world—Loyal, Madeline, and Patty.

Maybe they were unlikely people to be bound together by strains of music and circumstance, but it felt like they all belonged with each other in this time and place.

Loyal sang a few more songs, hymns mostly, and Madeline listened, curious. Surprised that his anger and bitterness at what had happened hadn't stopped him from choosing music that would honor the King.

She found herself curious about it, wanting to know more. That, along with the attraction, and her odd reaction to his touch, and the hope that she'd had twice today that he'd kiss her, scared her.

She didn't belong in Missouri. She loved the state, and the people were great, but her life was in LA, and when that was over, she'd always planned on going back to her family in England.

She'd never even considered living in a rural area, and on a farm no less, which was exactly where Loyal belonged, with his horses and his fields and all the things he did.

"I think she's asleep," Loyal said, his voice a bare whisper of sound.

Madeline didn't answer, but slid slowly out of the bed and walked to the door, waiting for Loyal before they both walked through, closing it softly behind.

Once in the hall, Madeline started to walk toward her room, but a touch on her arm stopped her, and she lifted her head and looked at Loyal as he stared down at her, a beam of moonlight slanting across his face, illuminating the scars, the twisted skin, and the mangled features.

Maybe in the darkness he couldn't tell where her eyes went, and she stared at his deformity like she hadn't before, examining it and cataloguing it. She thought about the pain and the horror that night as a child died. Loyal's child.

She wanted with all her heart to know what happened, but she couldn't ask. That absolutely had to be a story he gave her freely.

His hand didn't drop from her arm, but his fingers, long and warm, slid around and held it loosely. She wanted to move closer, but she stood, waiting.

"I heard your conversation the first night you were here. The one where you were talking to someone called Cheryl, and you admitted that you couldn't cook, didn't know what you're going to do. I think I can help you. I would like to help you. You've done so much for me. Please, let me."

Her eyes widened, and she gasped. All this time, when she'd wondered if he'd been hinting, or suspected, or just thought he was expecting her to say something...it had been true. He had known almost from the beginning. From that very first night.

She couldn't be angry. He'd kept her secret. And now he wanted to help.

"I think you probably can," she said. "Cheryl and I had a system worked out where she watched what I was doing and I had an earbud in my ear where I could hear her helping me know what to do while I did the goofy, quirky act in front of the camera." Her eyes had dropped, and she couldn't look at him. Because basically she was admitting that everything that she stood for was a lie.

She was ashamed.

"You guys are basically a team, and you were the head and the face, and she guided from behind the scenes." His voice held a note of humor. "Do you realize how applicable that is for us? Me with my face? Not wanting to be in front of the camera, and you perfect for it."

"You don't *want* to be. You could do it."

Maybe she shouldn't have said it, because she could feel him stiffen beside her. "You, with your perfect face, your gorgeous eyes that sparkle with life and happiness, those dimples that give you a little-girl cuteness, and a smile that makes a man want to do anything to see it again, it's easy for you to stand in front of the camera." His fingers tightened just a little on her arm before they loosened again and his thumb moved over her skin, causing her to shiver. "If you looked like me, it would be a different story."

He stepped forward a little more, and his other hand came up to her arm, and he spoke. "You know, you're not hiding the ugliness that I have, but you are hiding your secret. You wouldn't want to parade that out in front of everyone and let them all see it. You're very careful to keep it tucked away. You can't knock me for wanting to do the same with my physical features. Because they're even uglier than the secret you're hiding."

"No, it's not. Because I'm hiding a lie. You're pushing away the truth. You got those scars honorably. Unlike the lie I have."

"You're not lying to people. People think you can cook, but you're not telling them you can. You're entertaining them, bringing a smile, cheering people up. There's a profit." His hands slid up to her shoulders, and this time, she did step forward without really thinking about it.

Her hands came up and touched either side of his waist, lightly, gauging his reaction before they settled more fully on him.

"Look at what you've done to me. For me. Look at Patty. You've made my heart full, and I never thought I'd even know that I had a heart again." He stopped. "But that's not the reason I want to kiss you tonight." He didn't flinch or look away, and she stared up at him. "I never thought I would say that to anyone again. But it's true. I want to kiss you."

"You've been teasing me about it all night, and I've been waiting. Is this a tease, or is this a truth?" she asked.

Maybe she was flirting a little, maybe her words were lighter against his more serious, darker, and deeper ones. But his deep words and her light words reflected their personalities and somehow complemented each other, twisting, turning, and pulling them together until her arms were somehow around his neck and his were around her waist and running up her back, and his head lowered, and she lifted hers up.

The darkness and the moonlight were witnesses, silent and sweet, as his lips touched hers and her world shifted and spun and her breath caught and her heart pounded and her hands buried in his hair and her body pressed to his, the warmth turning to heat and the heat to sparks that turned into flames that drowned out everything except the man in front of her with his lips on hers and his hands on her back, pulling her closer, wanting what she wanted, needing the exact same thing she did.

Madeline's hands slid from the back of his head and cupped his cheeks. He jerked back.

For a second, her fingers had been on his scars which had felt soft and ridged like a supple plastic, not like skin. She hadn't meant to touch them. She'd just been so lost in his kiss.

And now, standing bereft in front of him, her lungs gasping, her lips tingling, and her heart hurting, she waited.

Was he angry?

Would he withdraw?

She supposed the direction that they took in their relationship, if what they had was called a relationship, was now up to him. Would he trust her?

"I am sorry."

She waited, unsure as to what he was apologizing for.

His shoulders moved up and down like he still hadn't quite gotten his breath under control. That pleased her, since she wanted to reach out and steady herself because of the shaking of her legs.

Despite the abrupt ending, it was the best kiss she'd ever had. The only kiss that had completely turned her brain off and left her unable to do anything but feel and respond.

It didn't even surprise her, either, because the attraction between them had been obvious to her from the beginning.

Though he was quiet and not effusive, it had also been obvious to her that he was a man with deep feelings and passions. All she had to do was watch his face as he looked at his daughter to know that much. Love, protection, devotion. It was all there. Deep and strong and exactly what a man should feel for his child.

How could she not admire that?

How could she not feel special when he turned all that depth of emotion toward her just now? With all of the focus and intensity she'd known he was capable of.

But it probably didn't mean anything. Passion was one thing. It didn't make a relationship. In fact, it was a poor basis for a relationship. Passion and attraction eventually burned out.

Just because she actually liked him, the man, his compassion, his humor when he allowed it to show, the devotion he had for his daughter, even the way he knew he was bitter at God and knew he needed to fix it, didn't mean that there could be anything more between them. Anyone who could admit that was worth admiring, but admiring was a long way from what she'd been thinking.

He shifted his hand, moving like it might come up, then dropped it back down to his side. "Does your silence mean I'm not forgiven?"

"No. My silence means I'm not sure what you were apologizing for?" She searched his eyes, wishing there was more light because she couldn't tell what he was thinking.

"It's true that I haven't kissed anyone in a long time, but I don't usually end things quite that precipitously. That was what the apology was for." There was an edge of humor in his voice but a touch of insecurity as well.

She stepped closer, closing the distance between them again as their bodies just brushed and she looked up. "As long as the apology wasn't for the kiss, I forgive you."

She didn't have any trouble seeing his teeth flash in the moonlight.

"Why would I apologize for the best kiss I've ever had in my life?" His hand came up and cupped her cheek.

Holding his eyes, she raised her hand and imitated the motion on his cheek. The one with the scars.

She didn't miss his flinch nor the setting of his jaw, as his body became like a great statue. Only his eyes, deep and dark and intensely focused on her, were alive.

Lightly, she ran her fingers over the ridges and swirls. Hard underneath, not supple, but soft, with none of the ridges and hair of regular skin. Such an odd feel, and fascinating.

He held still as she moved her hand, allowing her.

"I want to know the story."

His eyes closed. "Someday. Not tonight. Please."

Her heart fell a little, because she thought it was him not trusting her. But he kept speaking. "My daughter fell asleep in my arms for the first time in two years, and I had the best kiss of my life tonight. Don't make me relive old memories, the hard ones, and ruin all that. Just let me enjoy the afterglow for a little bit." He smiled. "We can talk about what we'll do with you and your cooking show. Make plans. We ought to get some groceries, whatever you're going to be making on the show, and practice. Tomorrow. It's January and my slow time of the year, and all I have to do is feed the animals and move some hay around."

"Are you sure?" She couldn't believe he was really going to help her. Even though he wouldn't be anywhere near cameras, his contract stated that he didn't even have to be in the house. He wanted to be far away from it that badly.

"Yes. I'm being serious. Let's get a plan together."

"Does the plan include kissing?" She wasn't a shy person, but that was bold, even for her, as her hand cupped his cheek and smoothed over the scar, hurting for the pain and the loss and the child he couldn't save.

He huffed a laugh. "It probably shouldn't, because if you hadn't moved your hand, I think I'd still be standing here kissing you."

"And I'd be standing here kissing you back and enjoying every minute."

"That way leads to trouble."

That was a perfect opening, and she didn't really feel like she was pushing when she said, "Where exactly is this leading?"

There were a few beats of silence as they stared at each other, neither one of them having an answer for that question.

Finally, he said, "Maybe we don't have to make a decision about that right now?" His fingers slid down her arm and grabbed her hand. "Maybe we can just be together and enjoy that for now, and make decisions about our future sometime in the future?"

It didn't really satisfy her, because she wanted to know, wanted to know what he thought and felt and was expecting, but it wasn't really fair for her to push, because she didn't know those things about herself.

"So we're together?" she asked, not even sure what that meant exactly.

"I'm with you." She could hear his breath suck in between his teeth. "My wife cheated on me. I guess trust is going to be hard for me to give.

But I've never been able to do more than one at a time. If I'm with you, I'm not going to be looking at anybody else." He sighed and looked away. "I want the same from you, but I don't know if I can trust you to give it to me."

"Then I guess I'll just have to show you. Because I'm the same. Just one."

"You make that sound simple."

"That part is. It's the idea that you live on a farm in Missouri and I'm not a farm girl that makes things tough for me."

"Not a farm girl, not horse rider." His hand came back. "I felt the bump on your head. You don't have a headache or anything?"

"No. It went away. I feel fine. I think it just scraped the skin in such a way that it bled a lot. Now it's good." She closed her eyes as his fingers probed around her head, even touching the lump in a way that didn't hurt, so gently and carefully. That gentleness pulled at her heartstrings more than anything else, that someone so big and strong could be so careful with her.

If she didn't watch it, she could end up falling in love with this man.

Chapter 16

Of course, Loyal's brother Clark was in the feed store with his wife Marlowe, the feed store manager, the next morning when Loyal walked in, holding Patty's hand in one of his and Madeline's hand with the other.

Clark's brows went up like a rocket on steroids, and he, not even trying to be inconspicuous, hit his wife on the arm and said in a stage whisper, "Is that my brother?"

"You're not even funny, Clark. Shut up."

Then Marlowe's eyes widened, and her brows seemed to be attached to the same rocket that Clark's were, but she smacked her husband before hurrying around the counter and giving Patty a big smile.

"I think this is our niece?" she asked as she stopped in front of them, smiling at Patty. "I can't believe how much you've grown, sweetheart. I'm your Aunt Marlowe, if you don't remember me." She held her hand out just like Patty was an adult, which made Patty feel special, if her puffed-out chest was any indication, and she shook Marlowe's hand solemnly.

"When is she gonna rub off on you?" Loyal asked Clark.

"I'm the one that needs to rub off on her. I'm working on it." Clark came around the counter and shook Patty's hand as well. "I'm Uncle Clark. The older and wiser brother."

Patty's eyes furrowed a little, like maybe she was trying to remember, but she grinned. Kids usually loved Clark. He was often a goofball they could relate to.

"So did you just come in here to visit and show off your new girl, who you have yet to introduce us to, or did you really want something?" Clark asked before he turned to Madeline and held out his hand. "I'm Clark. The handsome brother."

Madeline pulled her hand from Loyal's and shook Clark's. "Nice to meet you. I'm Madeline, and I'm with the smart brother."

Loyal huffed a laugh and put an arm around Madeline's shoulders. He couldn't keep from grinning down at her.

She was just being goofy, and he appreciated her taking his brother's teasing in the light spirit that it was meant, giving it back, and defending him all in the same breath. It gave him a sweet-good feeling deep inside.

Marlowe and Madeline chatted some, about the baby that Marlowe was expecting and a few other things that he didn't hear, while he was telling Clark that he wanted a bucket of minerals for his horses.

After they'd stood there for five or ten minutes, he and Clark had actually started talking about the crops for next year and some of the changes they wanted to make, so when Patty started to get restless, and Marlowe left to wait on other customers in the store, Madeline leaned over and said, "It's warm out for January, I'm going to take her to the park that I saw just up the street. Come and get us when you're done."

He stopped talking to Clark and leaned down, kissing Madeline's temple with a naturalness that surprised him. Being with her felt so right. "Thank you. I won't be very long."

She waved at Clark and Marlowe while Patty grabbed her hand and skipped out of the store behind her.

"You sure picked a looker, Loyal," Clark said before the door was even completely shut behind them.

Had he picked her? He wasn't sure. He thought maybe they picked each other.

"Go ahead. You can say, 'Loyal, you're ugly, what are you doing with a good-looking woman?'" He said it with a grin and not very much bitterness at all, because he knew Clark had meant it that way. But Clark was his brother and wouldn't hesitate to tease him about it.

THE BEAST GETS HIS COWGIRL IN THE SHOW ME STATE 145

"Okay. You're ugly. What are you doing with a good-looking woman?"

"Gable. You apologize this second." Marlowe's voice came from the far corner of the store.

Loyal grinned. "Somebody's in trouble. Gonna be sleeping on the couch tonight." He chuckled, and only a little bit of evilness entered the sound.

"Shut up." Clark tried to frown, but it was an expression his face didn't shift into naturally, and he ended up grinning instead. "I just said exactly what he told me to," he called back across to his wife. He lowered his voice. "Marlowe would be down to get me anyway. She doesn't like sleeping by herself."

Loyal nodded, wondering. He hadn't exactly meant to make a statement with Madeline by bringing her into town today and holding her hand. But he realized he had. Now he just wasn't sure what to do with it. And then Clark's comment about married people made him wonder how Madeline felt about it. About marriage, but also...the question teased his mind...was she a snuggler?

He didn't even let himself go down that train of thought.

Marriage.

He'd been there once and gotten burned badly. He hadn't forgotten that pain, which had been worse than the physical pain of his burns. The pain of having someone who'd vowed to stand beside him for the rest of his life come from another man's bed and stand across from him with the body of their dead son between them.

He still couldn't think about that without fire clutching his chest and seizing the back of his neck, scraping up and down and making him feel like he was being torn apart.

That's what it was. They'd become one in front of the preacher, and a part of him had been torn off and left when Lisa walked out. Not that he still loved her, just that they had been joined.

He wasn't sure he wanted to go through that again. He wasn't even sure whether he had enough to offer someone to make it worth their while to go through that again. He hadn't felt whole since she left. But maybe that had to do with the fire and his son and the pain and the scars and losing Patty as well. His whole family had blown up in his face that night.

He shoved that aside as he and Clark started to talk about the new corn seed that they were thinking of planting on the bottom hundred acres of the old farm.

MADELINE SAT ON A BENCH in the park. There were several other children there, and Patty had been a little shy at first, but now she played on the monkey bars laughing and chatting with them.

Off to the right a man and his two teenage sons tossed a frisbee to each other. It was fun to watch them, because they were good at it and quite skillful. They laughed and seemed to be enjoying each other's company as well.

That was the thing about small towns. The relaxed atmosphere, everybody seemed to know everyone else and if not like them, at least know them and get along with them.

As Madeline sat on the bench, soaking up the surprisingly warm winter sun, a feeling like she belonged here stole over her. Surprising her.

She'd never thought of herself as a small town, rural America, girl. But there was something about the feeling of everyone-pulling-for-everyone-else and acceptance, that made her feel peaceful and right.

Patty had just finished hanging upside down by her legs on the monkey bars when Madeline was startled out of her contemplation by a frisbee flying just in front of her and landing just to the side of a park bench.

She leaned forward to get up and grab it when a man jogged by in front of her, grabbing it and tossing it, before turning to her. "Sorry about that. A gust of wind grabbed it and we weren't expecting it. It didn't hit you did it?"

"No." Madeline leaned back on the bench. "I've been admiring how much fun you guys seem to be having. It's enjoyable to watch people who really know what they're doing. It's obvious you guys have done this before."

"Yeah. Ever since their mom died this is kind of our thing that we do just to get us out of the house and doing something together." The man planted his feet, but his hands seemed unable to be still and he rubbed the back of his neck.

Madeline nodded, wondering if she should offer condolences for the death of his wife. He didn't seem overly sad as she looked at him. Square jaw with just a day's worth of stubble on it, and a face that would do well in Hollywood. His hands looked like a working man's hands, though, and she guessed his job had him outside.

"Sorry about your wife."

He tilted his head, as though thinking about her words, and then he said. "It's been a while. We've adjusted." He jerked his head toward the swing set and continued, "I thought that looked like Loyal Hudson's little girl, and I thought I'd come over and ask you about her."

Immediately Madeline was on alert. This guy seemed harmless enough, but her job was to protect Patty, and she would protect Loyal as well, if she felt like there was any threat. Not that he needed her to. That's just how she felt.

"It is." Her words were a little short, and she definitely had put, if not physical distance, mental distance between them.

"It's okay. I don't want to talk to her or anything. I just happened to be fire chief, and I was there the night Loyal's house burned down."

Madeline's whole attitude changed. She wanted him to tell her everything. She tried to stop the questions in her brain and pick the most important one. "Can you tell me about it?"

"Depends." The guy's eyes came back to her, and they seem to assess her, with consideration. "Why do you have her?"

What should she say to that? She wanted to give the whole story, but it was too long. "I've been there to help ease the transition between Patty leaving her mum and staying with her dad. I guess the memories are so bad that she couldn't stand to be in the same room with Loyal without crying. I seem to help that. And Lisa allowed her to stay for the first time since the fire. Loyal doesn't talk about it, and I don't want to go behind his back, but I am curious." There. That was as honest as she could be without going into unnecessary detail.

The guy held out his hand. "My name's Andrew, by the way."

She shook it. "Madeline."

"I thought so. I've heard rumors about the celebrity chef that's around, and being that I do the cooking for my family, or at least I was in charge of teaching my boys to cook and of feeding them at times, I've watched a few things on the food network. Your show is my favorite." His look turned sheepish. "I feel like you're just like me, a little inept in the kitchen, although it can't be true, since you have your own show."

If he only knew.

Madeline just pressed her lips together to keep her grin from being too guilty and nodded. "Thanks."

The guy crossed his arms over his chest and turned so his back was to the rest of the park. His voice lowered.

"Loyal brought his daughter out of the fire first. He went back in for his son. That's when the burning beam fell on him. I tried to keep him from going back in. But I wasn't any match for a man who was as desperate as Loyal was to save his son. He loved his kids."

Andrew looked off in the approximate direction of Patty, although Madeline had the feeling he wasn't seeing her.

"The house wasn't fully engulfed when he went back in, but it was close. Although the child – his son who was still in a crib – died of smoke inhalation. He couldn't save him, but Loyal brought the body out; he was on fire." Andrew stopped speaking, and the silence beat between them for a bit.

Finally Andrew seem to shake himself, and said, "I want to say he was a brave man, but I just think he was a man who loved his child. Not being able to save his kid probably wasn't as hard, though, as knowing that the fire was most likely his fault, since it started in the kitchen. The scars that he has, have changed him, but I don't think as much as the events of that night."

Andrew breathed out and turned, no longer shutting out the rest of the playground.

Madeline got the feeling the story was over. What more was there to say?

"Thanks so much for telling me."

"Sure. I was surprised to see Patty, but hopeful, when I saw that she was with you. I grew up with Loyal, and he's a good man. But he pretty much lost everything he loved that night. Including his wife. But that part isn't for me to tell."

Just the way Andrew looked made Madeline curious. She'd already been curious about Loyal, and she hoped that eventually he'd tell her what went on. But there was a sadness, almost a haunted look in Andrew's eyes that said his easy words about his wife and his children's adjustment after her death didn't begin to scratch the surface of the story that he had to tell.

He chatted a bit about the weather, before he said, "I better get back to my boys. Thanks for talking."

A moment later he ran off.

Just a few minutes later Loyal came walking down the sidewalk. Andrew stopped and talked to him for a few minutes, before Loyal walked on, coming over and dropping down beside her on the bench, with his arm around her, comfortable and easy. A definite change from the way he'd been even a week ago.

What hadn't changed was the way he made her feel. Excitement and anticipation and an easy familiarity that made her wish they could sit here together forever.

She was tempted to broach the subject that Andrew had just spoken about, but she didn't want to ruin the good feelings that surrounded them, so she kept her mouth shut and just enjoyed the day, because she knew her time with Loyal was limited.

Chapter 17

"Go ahead and sprinkle it all over the pan, honey." Loyal watched as Patty stood on a chair next to him at the bar and sprinkled cheese over the top of the pan of chicken that Patty and Madeline had just put together under his instruction.

It was obvious that Madeline had gotten good at following audible directions, and her personality had really come out while they'd made this.

He understood why people enjoyed her show. She wasn't afraid to make fun of herself, and whatever was in her head seemed to come out her mouth, in a way that could make anyone laugh. He'd had a good time.

"I'm pretty confident we can do this," he said.

Her eyes shot up to meet his, smiling and reflecting the excitement that he felt. "Me too. Part of the reason that Cheryl and I have been so successful is there's just some kind of connection there. I feel the same thing with you." Her mouth closed, almost as though she wasn't going to say anymore, but then the next words came out. "Only stronger."

He thought he knew what she meant and some of the excitement that he'd felt, dimmed. He wasn't sure how badly he wanted to feel a connection with anyone else. In his experience, it only meant pain.

But he remembered what she'd said about throwing oneself out there, not worrying about how badly it hurt. He knew that was the right way to do it, just do right and let the Lord handle the rest. To not build a protective shell around himself which effectively blocked him off from the people in his life.

He'd been thinking about it after their talk, not just about Madeline, although she was always the one who was at the forefront of what he was thinking, but about his family and the town in general. Just because he'd been hurt, burned, literally, didn't mean that God was done with him, nor that it was okay for him to hide in his house or farm, afraid of that same pain, or worse.

He kept a hand on Patty, so she wouldn't fall out of her chair, but he leaned behind her toward Madeline, intending to place a kiss on her cheek.

She shifted slightly, and his lips ended up brushing hers. His daughter was busy concentrating on getting the cheese just right, but it still wasn't the time for him to kiss Madeline the way he wanted to.

Still, his body didn't quite agree, and it was longer than he intended before he pulled back with her taste on his tongue and his breath and his heartbeat racing. He watched as her eyes opened, a smile on her lips and her green eyes sparkling.

"More?" she asked softly.

He grinned. It was exactly how he felt.

Her eyes went to Patty, before she smirked a little, like she knew more was impossible, but wanting him to know she wanted it anyway.

"Later?" he asked, low enough that he didn't think Patty would question what he was saying.

She nodded.

His smile widened, and they shared a look that he felt the whole way from his head to his toes and every place in between.

Maybe this is what it felt like to fall in love?

Wanting to be with her all the time. Thinking about her all the time. Enjoying her company, no matter what they were doing. Feeling confident that she wasn't with him for any material gain, and that she didn't care about the physical scars that had changed his life.

But, more importantly, that she did care about the scars no one could see.

Maybe it was time for him to talk to Madeline about everything that had happened.

THE BEAST GETS HIS COWGIRL IN THE SHOW ME STATE

A knock on the door startled him.

He glanced at Patty, who had half the cheese spread. He didn't see any point in rushing her. If she wanted to take her time and do good job, he was fine with that.

"Mind if I get this?"

"No. Go right ahead." Madeline, too, didn't seem to be inclined to hurry Patty. "I think I can put this in the oven when she's done. I might not remember to check the time when I do it though." One side of her mouth pulled back, and she lifted her shoulder in a little bit of an apology.

"Don't worry about it. We'll figure it out."

It wasn't until he'd walked away from her that he actually thought to wonder who in the world would be at the door.

His mother probably would have tapped the door before she walked in and called out his name. His brothers wouldn't have even done that much. They'd have just walked in.

That left room for a lot of other people, but his gut told him that his ex-wife was on the other side.

She'd mentioned wanting to take Patty home today the last time they'd talked on the phone. He'd put her off. At least he thought he had.

He opened the door. She hadn't been put off.

"Loyal," Lisa said, her nose tilted slightly in the air. "Do you have Patty ready to go?"

"I haven't seen her for two years. Surely I get longer than a day with her?"

"I had plans, things I want to do. I didn't realize she was going to be okay staying here. We'll plan you into our next visit."

"When's that going to be?" He really should get a lawyer. He didn't want to fight, but he wanted his fair time with his daughter.

"This spring. Relax. I'll be in over the summer too."

"If you get her all winter, I should get her in the summer."

Lisa huffed. "I didn't come here to argue with you about this. I just want my daughter, and I want to leave. Let's not make this ugly."

He didn't want to make it ugly. He didn't want to fight in front of Patty. But he did want to be able to be with his daughter. He'd been passive long enough. Lisa had taken advantage of him when he hadn't felt well and couldn't fight. And as much as he didn't like to argue and fight, he would do it for his daughter.

But not in front of her.

Patty fussed some, as they gathered up her things. It gratified him to know that she didn't want to leave, but he didn't use that to his advantage, because he wouldn't use his daughter as a weapon to hurt his ex.

Thankfully Madeline picked up on that too and imitated his words of encouragement that Patty would enjoy whatever Lisa had planned and that she could come back.

Still, when Patty left, it was like a part of him had been taken away, and he just needed to be alone.

He and Madeline cleaned up the kitchen in silence.

Finally, he said, "I'm going to the barn for a bit. You can text me if you need me."

He didn't invite her to go, because he didn't really want her. He already thought about her way too much and wanted to be with her constantly.

But he didn't want to make the same stupid mistake twice. He'd already married someone who was beautiful and successful and look what that got them. Nothing but heartache.

He put his hat and boots on and walked out the door.

THE BEAST GETS HIS COWGIRL IN THE SHOW ME STATE

MADELINE WAITED UNTIL after dark to go out to the barn and look for Loyal. She reasoned he needed time for himself. She could imagine how difficult it was to try to "share" a child.

She couldn't blame Lisa entirely, because Lisa was going through just as big of a difficulty, and Madeline was sure that Lisa loved her child just as much as Loyal did. Madeline hoped if it were her in that position, she would be fair with the time they spent with their child, because from where she was standing, it looked to her like Lisa was really pushing her advantage, and cutting Loyal out as much as she could.

Still, a parent's love for their child might drive them to do whatever it took to be able to spend as much time with them as they could.

Even if it meant sacrificing their integrity, as Lisa had, in order for them to get what they wanted.

But she was all team Loyal, and she hurt because he hurt. Having Patty, and getting to know her again, had relaxed Loyal and made him smile easier and more freely than he had since she'd come.

Maybe he wouldn't welcome her presence now, but she wanted to make sure he was okay. He'd been out for hours, and when the sun went down, it got cold. He'd walked out without a coat.

When she walked into the barn, she could tell he'd been working. Everything was cleaned up and swept and looked neat and freshly oiled or cleaned or whatever one did with the tack on the wall, that shone with freshness and care.

The lights were on, and she assumed Loyal was in there somewhere, but as she looked around she couldn't see him.

Not wanting to startle him, she said, "Loyal?"

"Over here." He answered her right away. She assumed he wasn't angry at her, just needed time for himself. Still, she moved carefully.

Looking around, she walked forward and finally saw him in the stall beside M&M.

"She's in labor."

Madeline didn't say anything, but went to his side and looked between the bars that separated the stalls.

M&M was on her feet, but she seemed distracted, and her sides heaved. After a little while her whole body stiffened, and she seemed to bear down, although Madeline didn't see that her bearing down was affecting anything.

"She just started pushing not too long ago. Before that I was coming in." He looked over at her. "Honest."

"I believe you. I realized you needed some time. But I wanted to make sure you're okay. I don't have to stay."

"I'd appreciate it if you would. I kind of wanted to talk to you."

He wanted to talk to her? Her mouth hung open, as she stared at him. Fear and anxiety warred with excitement and anticipation in an uncomfortable and sharp battle in her chest.

Was he going to tell her that them being together was a mistake? After dealing with Lisa today, maybe he didn't want to ever have to deal with that again. Or maybe, and she hoped, he decided he was going to tell her the things that she'd asked and he'd asked for her to wait.

"Are you mad at me because I came out without saying anything?"

It hadn't even occurred to her to get mad. But she wondered, because of his question, if maybe it was something that Lisa would've gotten upset over.

Maybe if Madeline hadn't seen so clearly how bad he was hurting, she would be annoyed that he hadn't told her exactly where he was going and how long he'd be gone. "You don't owe me that information."

Her words made his head turn quickly, and his eyes were intense as they looked at her. "I think I do. And I didn't give it to you. I'm sorry. I asked if you were mad."

"No."

He seemed to relax a little. His eyes dropped, and he looked back at the horse.

THE BEAST GETS HIS COWGIRL IN THE SHOW ME STATE

"Lisa told me she was going to her mother's house to stay, the night of the fire. I was cooking in the kitchen, and finished up, and was going to put the kids to bed. As I picked up Patty, I guess, because I don't really know, for sure, but somehow I think I knocked the pile of hot pads on top of the burner I'd just been using and didn't notice. I put my son in his crib after feeding him a bottle, and I sang to Patty for a while, rocking her in the chair before I put her in bed too."

He sighed, a long drawn out sound, and ran his hand through his hair, shifting on his feet, before gripping the bars with both hands tight, his knuckles white.

"You have no idea how many times I wish I would've gone down and out through the kitchen. But that house had a set of back stairs, and I took them down and went out the back room without ever paying any attention. I had a horse in labor, and I wanted to check on her. So I went out as soon as I put the kids down." He swallowed, loud in the silence.

"The mare looked just like this, pushing, but the foal hadn't emerged." His head nodded at M&M, still laboring in the stall beside them. Occasionally her ears flicked, like she was listening to the soothing timbre of Loyal's voice. "I stood for a while watching her." He shook his head, his face pinched and painful. "I don't even know why, but I just felt like I needed to go back to the house. Normally, I would have stayed there until she had her foal, and it was breathing on its own. But I just felt the need to go back to the house."

He closed his eyes, and she put her hand on his arm. His whole body shook when she touched him, like ripples in a pond when a rock has been thrown in. But he didn't move away from her. His hand came up and settled over top of hers. Her hand shifted, and their fingers threaded together.

He lifted her hand to his mouth and kissed her knuckles.

"When I went outside all I could see were flames. That's all that's in my head right now. The house must have been there, because I went in, but there were just flames everywhere. I called 911 right away, then dropped my phone, as I went to get the kids."

His voice trailed off, and Madeline shifted closer, feeling like he needed comfort, knowing he did, but not knowing how to give it to him.

Was there comfort that could help anyone with a wound like his?

She didn't think so. It was probably something he would always live with. Nothing she could do about it.

After a long time, during which M&M went through at least two contractions, Loyal finally spoke again.

"Patty was the easiest to get to, and even then, when I first went in, I knew getting my son was going to be risky. I didn't want to not save Patty, whom I could get to easily."

Madeline's breath came in short gasps and her stomach clenched into a tight, little ball. She bit her lip, wanting to ask him to not tell her, sure she didn't want to know anymore.

But she leaned against him and his arm came around her, his voice going over her head.

"I carried her down first. It took maybe ten seconds. But I needed her to stay outside, and there was no one there to keep her." He shifted and she looked up. His eyes were tortured when they looked at her. "I had to scare her. I had to make her understand that she could not go back in the house. Not for anything. She was crying and clinging to me and I couldn't take the time to comfort her. I couldn't take the time to explain to her, even if she could have understood. She was only five. She just wanted me. And her mom."

At that he paused, his eyes falling to the floor, going to the side maybe a little. "I yelled at her. I screamed in her face that she was not to move. I threatened her. It was for her own good. I couldn't stand it if she'd have gone back in the house looking for me."

"It's okay," Madeline said softly. "You did what you needed to. I don't know what else you could have done. She would have followed you if you hadn't. Of course she would have. She didn't want to be outside alone in the dark by herself with the big scary fire in front of her and her daddy gone."

He nodded, his eyes closed. "I had no idea that fear would last for years."

M&M made a noise and he looked back at the straining horse. "I think someone else had already called the fire department. Someone had seen the flames before I did. I don't even know. I was in the hospital for a long time and I'm sure I heard stories, but any rate, by that time, after I yelled at Patty and scared her on purpose, before I was sure she wouldn't follow me, the firetrucks had pulled up. Someone took her and Andrew grabbed a hold of me, begging me not to go back in. But I couldn't live with myself if I didn't go in and, if necessary, lose my life saving my son."

She'd known that was the kind of person he was. It wasn't hard to see he wouldn't stand outside and watch his house burn down around his baby.

"He trusted me to keep him safe and I failed him. He was already dead when I got to his crib. Smoke inhalation they said later. I guess babies can't handle..."

His voice trailed off, like talking about the cause of death was just too much. "I brought his body out, and by that time Lisa was there. She hadn't been at her mother's."

His jaw clenched, obviously this was upsetting for him as well, but she didn't see pain as much as she saw anger. "She'd been with her boyfriend. I held our son, and she stood and blamed me for everything."

M&M let out a shrill whinny, and they both looked over. Little hooves had appeared, two of them, pointing straight ahead. "The foal's in the right position," Loyal said softly. "We should see a nose lying between them next."

Madeline didn't say anything. She'd never seen an animal born, and she was awed, although her heart was aching and heavy, each beat feeling tough like it was encased in rubber.

"I couldn't even get angry at her, because she was right. The fire was all my fault."

"If she had been there she would have known the house was on fire and the children could have been taken out immediately and been safe." Madeline's words rushed out soft, out of respect for the labor that M&M was going through, but anger laced her tone.

"I know. That doesn't negate the fact the fire was my fault, and I'd only been able to save one of my children."

"I talked to Andrew at the park. He said a burning beam fell on you." She hoped she wasn't out of line, but she wanted him to know that she knew. He had not mentioned it at all.

"Yeah. I guess I didn't even notice. I mean of course I noticed, but I didn't care. All that mattered was that I protected my son. He didn't have a single burn mark on him."

He did what needed to be done. Obviously. And he hadn't been able to do any more than he could. For whatever reason, it hadn't been the Lord's will that his son survive.

Saying that wouldn't be any comfort to Loyal though. Madeline knew it. He probably didn't understand any better than she did why God allowed bad things to happen to good people. Why babies died, and wives who cheated weren't punished.

But she didn't need to say anything, because he said, "The pain of my son's death will always hurt. I'll live the rest my life with that." His hand squeezed hers, as his other hand held onto the bar. "But I can see that there might be a plan B in this, as hard as it is. And maybe I need to look beyond myself to see it." He turned his head to look at her, like she somehow had something to do with that, even though she knew she didn't.

"I can't believe you're not more upset with Lisa," she said, not meaning to stir up trouble, but that was what astonished her about the whole story. Lisa had been cheating on him, and he barely even mentioned it.

He lifted his shoulder. "I had a lot of time in the hospital to think about that. You can't make someone love you. You can't make someone stay. You can't make them be true. It has to be their choice."

Madeline understood. He was right.

"I'm not saying it doesn't hurt, and I'm not saying it's not hard, and I'm not saying I want to go through it again," his gaze was directed overhead to the shadows in the stall on the other side of M&M. "I think you can only be responsible for you. Lisa has a lack of character, but it isn't my fault. I can't fault her love for her children, because she loved her kids just as much as I did, and she wants the best for them, even if what she thinks is the best is different than what I do."

Madeline blinked, trying to process the maturity behind that statement. She supposed he could have lain in the hospital, angry and getting more bitter every day at Lisa, and he hadn't. It sounded like he'd managed to forgive her. Even if he had put up walls, and retreated behind them, and been afraid to put himself out there and take risks at the same time, but who could blame him for that?

It was like he could read her mind, because he said, "Maybe I need a little time to heal emotionally as well. As much as I don't even want to admit that I have emotions." He grinned a little at that, the first smile she'd seen since Patty left. "But I think it's time I stop being a coward. Baby steps maybe."

Medeline admired the attitude and the thought even while something nagged in the back of her head. Something she should do. Obviously Loyal was facing his fears. Maybe she should too.

"This being with you," he held up their joined hands. "This is a huge step for me. I appreciate you seeing me beyond the front I put up, thinking that there might be something in here still worth taking a chance on." He tapped his chest.

"Worth loving." She said the words softly, not really thinking about it, but not wanting to take them back once they were out in the air, either.

His face twitched. She'd surprised him.

His eyes squinted, and he swallowed heavily. "Really? Worth loving?"

"I think so." She nodded. "In fact I know so."

The horse squealed again, and this time as she pushed a little nose appeared.

"It won't be long now. Once the head and shoulders are out, the rest will come out easily."

He was right, and it wasn't long until the new baby foal was on the ground, and M&M was up taking care of her baby.

Maybe it was the first birth that Madeline had ever witnessed, but she hardly thought the miracle of birth would ever get old. There was something so amazing about seeing a new life come into the world, or maybe the amazing thing was being able to share it with a man as honorable and as good as Loyal.

Chapter 18

It was funny how some things a person worries and frets about and they turn out to be nothing. Madeline considered this as the canned applause echoed through the house, and she held up the steaming chili and golden cornbread she'd just made.

The show couldn't have gone better.

"And that's a wrap," Stella said, a huge smile on her face, her phone in her hand. As she spoke, her thumbs started flying over the keypad. "If the social media response is any indication, this is the most popular show ever."

"You were brilliant. I'm sorry I was laughing so much. Don't be so funny and I'll have an easier time giving more instructions and doing less laughing." Loyal's voice came in her ear, the same as it had been the entire show.

Beloved voice.

It hadn't been that long since she'd heard it for the first time, but it had become familiar, and not only did it give her those tender-good feelings that went the whole way to her heart and back, but it belonged to someone who truly seemed to care about her.

Cheryl texted her a "congratulations it was awesome" message and Madeline sent a quick text back, but she could hardly wait to step into Loyal's arms. He was the one she really wanted to celebrate with. Because, instead of facing the world and losing everything she had, he not only helped her save that, but it sounded like he'd helped her move it up to a whole new level.

Not that she even cared, really. It was more the idea that he not only said he had her back, he actually had it.

He came down the stairs from where he'd been watching. He grinned and caught her, twirling her around before kissing her hard and long.

"Just give me a second, then you guys can have the rest of the night to yourselves." Stella's voice broke through, and Madeline pulled back, as Loyal lifted his head. She kept a hold on him, because as always, his kiss disoriented her.

Stella tapped a bit on her keypad before looking up. "Now I know you weren't going to want to stay around this rinky-dink town all week long between shows, considering that you won't have anything to do. So I rescheduled your charity work, that you were planning on doing anyway, to be done in St. Louis. Just a few hours' drive away. You'll spend the week there and come back here in time for a run through practice, and then the actual live taping. I've set every thing up, and I just emailed you the information." She gave her notebook one last tap then looked up, a genuine smile on her face. "I don't know how you do it, but you are brilliant. Keep up the good work."

Stella didn't take any more time to look at Madeline, as she walked away already answering another call. It was a good thing, because Madeline's mouth was hanging open, and she wasn't sure if she could have put a smile on her face and pretended to be happy about the charity work.

Normally she loved giving back and considered it a privilege that went along with the great blessing she'd been given. But she didn't want to do charity work. She wanted to be with Loyal.

He hadn't said, but she assumed he'd been thinking she was going to continue to stay with him for the next eight weeks, while they did the live show.

"You weren't expecting that." Loyal's voice brought her back to the present, and she closed her mouth with a snap. She could get it changed. After all, it wasn't hard to reschedule, and Madeline always had a say in it. Just because she had been planning on doing charity work didn't mean that she had to continue to do it. It could be canceled.

"Thank you. I would hate to think that you are assuming that I knew this all along, and it just got sprung on you." She turned with a smile as Loyal put his arm around her shoulders, looking down at her.

"I love that you're doing charity work. Maybe I can come see you in St. Louis. And it sounds like you'll be here at least for two days each week for the next eight weeks."

She nodded slowly. He didn't seem upset. Was he trying to make the best of it for her? Or was he relieved to have his house back?

Maybe this was for the best. Things were going kind of fast between Loyal and her anyway. It had barely been two weeks since they'd even met. Maybe her being gone and them only seeing each other a little bit would give them a chance to put the relationship into perspective.

They hadn't even admitted that they had a relationship.

"I think we were pretty good as a team." He grinned down at her, and she had to return a smile. She and Loyal clicked even better than Cheryl and she had. He was less serious, and she played off of that in her head, doing an even better job of entertaining the audience. It really had gone spectacularly well.

"I have to agree with that. I totally felt comfortable from the very first word and you are amazing. Thank you." She tried not to let the thoughts in her head show on her face. After all, there'd been no commitment. She assumed he was helping her for these eight weeks, and they hadn't said anything about any kind of permanence between them and their relationship, and they both probably assumed that Cheryl would be back and taking over her spot in Madeline's ear. So there had definitely been no permanence in working together, either.

Yes, she wasn't going to fight to stay. It was probably for the best that she would be going.

"I'd suggest we celebrate the great show with a horseback ride, but what seems like celebration to me would be more like torture for you."

"Actually, I was hoping I would get a chance to get back on a horse. I've always heard that if you fall off, you should get right back on."

She shoved all of those other thoughts aside. She wasn't big on living in the moment - she always had the future in mind - but in this regard, she couldn't change it, couldn't fix it, and didn't even know what it could be. It wasn't all up to her.

It would just have to fall out the way it did.

MADELINE COULDN'T BELIEVE it had been eight weeks.

Eight episodes of the most successful live cooking show in history. Her producers begged her to extend it and do more.

But with every show, she felt worse and worse.

Loyal seemed to be enjoying himself, and he handled what he did beautifully. She thought he might be getting a little bored though. She couldn't blame him. Even though she'd had her people put him on salary, and pay him generously, what he did with her wasn't exactly challenging. Although they always had a good time during the show. She laughed more then than she did all week long and he admitted he did too.

She hadn't asked him to continue. Even though the text that she had received two weeks ago from Cheryl had made her want to.

Cheryl had met up with an old flame from high school, not long before her mother had died. She'd fallen in love and wasn't coming back to the states.

They'd had a long, late-night conversation over it, and Madeline was thrilled for Cheryl and couldn't begrudge her any bit of happiness.

Which gave Madeline two choices.

She could ask Loyal to fill in Cheryl's spot. She had a feeling Loyal would do it. He'd been attentive and affectionate and had spent every spare second they had that they weren't taping that she was at the farm together. But they hadn't talked about their future.

Or she could do what she'd already decided she was going to do today.

It felt like there was a windstorm in her stomach, and she tried to settle it, in vain, since what she was doing in a few moments was a risk she had never been willing to take before.

But she couldn't live this life anymore.

After watching Loyal come out of the protective shell that he'd built up around himself, and take her into town, joking with people, and seeing the looks on their faces as they realized Loyal had become an almost completely new person, or maybe had become the person he was before the fire. It shocked people. And she loved seeing it.

But he was becoming more real, while she...hadn't grown at all. She still had her big secret, the one she protected with everything she had.

Not anymore. Standing behind the counter, she watched as the numbers clicked down" five, four, three, two, one and, "You're live!" Chad's finger pointed at her, and she placed a bright smile on her face.

"Good afternoon and welcome to Cooking in the Country with Madeline." She opened the way she always did, but then she broke from the script and what was expected. She didn't allow herself to look for Stella, and she ignored the instruction that Loyal had spoken in her earpiece.

"I have something that I need to confess to everyone. But first I want to thank everyone for a great two years. This has been the ride of my life. I've enjoyed every second. But, I have to admit, it's been a...lie.

"From the very first, my best friend, Cheryl, gave me every instruction it took in order to be able to put these recipes together. She created them, and she instructed me on making them, because," she paused. She supposed it ended up being a dramatic pause, but for her, it was a pause to gather herself so she would be able to say what she needed to say. "I can't cook."

Maybe, if she were thinking more clearly, she would picture the shocked gasps of her audience members as they tuned in and watched her show.

She did hear them from the camera crews, and from Stella.

But her focus was on her earpiece. "What are you doing?" Loyal's voice came through. "Why are you doing this? You're more successful now than you've ever been! What's going on?"

"I realized I couldn't live a lie anymore. I should have done this to begin with. I should have been honest. Maybe it was just acting. Maybe it was just me pretending to be something I wasn't, but people believed it." She held her hands up. "I make sure everyone knows that the lie was me. Only me. Cheryl knew about it, of course..." her voice trailed off. "And, to be clear, Cheryl and I split everything equally. Any success we had was as much her as it was me. We were equal partners. I was just the face."

Tempted to squirm, Madeline kept her hands still. "I can't take the lie anymore. I can't cook. And I'm not kidding. I can barely boil water. I might be able to make boxed macaroni and cheese if you don't mind it being gluey, which is kind of how I like it," she said.

A few titters from the camera guys told her that her audience might be laughing too, even though she was serious.

"We could have talked about this." Loyal's voice came in her ear again.

"I didn't want to be talked out of it." She said that to Loyal, then she looked in the camera. "I've fallen in love." She sighed. "I've fallen in love with a man who's honest and strong and brave. I've watched him grow and become better over the last two months I've known him, and I've admired him more every time I saw him."

She set her jaw, against the words that loyal was whispering in her ear. "You never said that to me. I had no idea."

"I'm saying it now," she said softly. "It's not just you. You inspired me, but this has been a huge stumbling block between me and the

THE BEAST GETS HIS COWGIRL IN THE SHOW ME STATE

Lord, as well. I can't tell you how freeing it is that there is no longer anything between me and my Savior."

Loyal was quiet. There wasn't anything he could say to that because he knew it to be true. Her lie stymied her relationship with Christ just as much as his bitterness. He'd overcome it. She needed to as well.

Turning her focus back to the cameras, she continued. "The man I love has given people who don't deserve it the benefit of the doubt, and where they earned what should have been hatred from him, he gave them grace. That takes bravery. Because when people hurt you, and you give them grace, it's not only exceptionally hard, it's like turning the other cheek, because, after all, they might do it again. How can I look at that kind of bravery and not be inspired? How can I see someone like that every day, and know how much I'm hiding, and how much I don't deserve to be with him?"

"Don't be ridiculous. It's never been a matter of whether or not you deserve me. It's always been the other way around. You are the one that's whole."

"What you look like has nothing to do with it," she said, speaking to Loyal. "What I look like has nothing to do with it. It's what I am. I've always wanted to be judged on my character rather than what I look like. It's my character that's ugly. Not anymore." She lifted her chin, looking straight into the cameras in case anyone missed it the first time. "I can't cook."

Loyal was talking, but she didn't listen. Reaching up, she pulled the ear bud out of her ear. She held it up. "This is how that man I was telling you about, the one that I've fallen in love with, tells me how to cook. Tells me what to do. Right down to telling me which bowl has peppers in it and which bowl has cucumbers. You might not believe it, but I can't tell the difference. Never could." She swept her hand over the all the bowls of things on the counter. "I'm not a chef. I'm just an actress. An actress who lies. And I'm done lying."

Maybe she should be crying here. She kind of thought, when she went over in her head the things she might say, that she might end up crying. But she didn't feel like crying. She felt free, and she hadn't even realized the weight that had been pushing down on her, strangling her with the guilt that she wasn't what she seemed.

"I know everyone is probably really disappointed to me. I'm sorry to let you all down. I suppose you'll understand, if I'm not available on social media for a while. Thanks so much for giving me the experience of my life."

She was about to turn away, walk off the set, when movement caught her eye.

Loyal.

Walking toward her.

She expected him to stop out of range of the cameras, but he didn't.

He didn't stop until he was beside her at the counter. He took her shoulders in both of his hands, and she was too shocked to resist as he turned her.

"Just for the record, I love you, too. I might have picked a more private place to say that for the first time," he looked around giving a nod at the cameras, "but I guess you're comfortable in front of these, and I'm not gonna let them keep me from you." He paused for just a second. "I mean it. Whatever baloney you were saying about not deserving me is just that. And I understand your guilt and your need to confess, but then you have to understand my need to be here beside you."

She couldn't believe he was out in front of the cameras. He had loosened, and become like his old self – the self before the fire – but she had never thought he would go to that extreme. There was no denying it, though, since his bad side was facing the cameras, and he didn't even seem to care.

"Now, we have all these ingredients out in front of us." His eyes swept the counter. "I think it'd be fun if we cook together. What do you think?"

She looked into his eyes, which were smiling down at her. This hadn't been how she'd pictured this playing out, but she couldn't deny that she liked it. She could go along with it.

"I think that sounds like fun." No one from the camera crew, nor Stella, cut them off, so they went with it. Loyal taking charge of the cooking, while she took charge of the commentary, and they balanced each other out beautifully, if the look on Stella's face was any indication as the show ended.

Stella talked animatedly, her phone to her ear, as the red light went off, and it was a wrap.

Loyal turned to her immediately, and pulled her to him, wrapping his arms around her and looking down at her. "That took some guts, girl."

"I could say the same thing to you. You didn't hesitate to walk in front of those cameras. I never imagined that you would."

"That's where you were. I had to be in the same place." He gave her a look. "Since you took me out of your ear."

He grinned. She couldn't help but to return it, feeling his words settle around her like a warm blanket. He wanted to be where she was. That was enough for her.

"Maybe this isn't the best time," he looked around the room. "But I feel like my life is finally coming together. Lisa's moving back here to be with her mom, and she's agreed to mediation, so we can figure out something that will work for us to share Patty between us. But that isn't everything I want anymore." His eyes looked down at her, and she couldn't have looked away even if she'd wanted to, which she didn't.

"I know you're probably never going to be a cowgirl, and you'd never wanted to be a farmer's wife, but I was hoping we could figure out something long-term that both of us could live with."

Long-term? What did he mean by that?

Maybe he saw the questions on her face.

"I wasn't clear, was I?" he pursed his lips, seeming to need a minute to gather his thoughts. "Probably because this is a pretty scary thing for me. I've been here once before, but not with someone like you. Would you marry me? We can figure everything out. That includes me giving up whatever I need to give up. I'll do it. I want to be with you."

So funny, because when she first met Loyal, she wouldn't have termed him a romantic person. But she couldn't picture anything more romantic than the proposal he'd just given her. He'd give up everything? Even his farm? Despite the fact that his daughter had just moved nearby? He'd give up being able to see her more often?

"What if I want to move back to England?"

His brows went up, as his breath pulled in. But he didn't hesitate more than half a second. "Then I'll buy plane ticket too. Or a boat ticket, since someone doesn't like to fly."

She grinned. "Really?"

He nodded. "Whatever it takes."

She bit her lip. "What if I want to be a cowgirl?"

"I suggest you don't quit your day job."

They laughed together. He said, "That would make me the happiest. But I can't expect to get everything. And that would pretty much do it."

"What if I said I wanted children?"

"I want that too."

She'd been worried that he might not want more children after what he'd gone through with the fire and losing a son. She hadn't really considered kids and family, but honestly, her career wasn't the most important thing anymore.

"I'd like to stay here. And that's a yes by the way."

He lowered his head and they kissed on it.

Epilogue

Zane Hudson slammed the door of his pickup closed. This would be his last single dads meeting before his girls arrived in Cowboy Crossing. Permanently, if his ex didn't fight the judge's new custody order.

Highly unlikely. But for now, his daughters were finally coming home.

The weight of years of struggles, court appearances, witnesses, private detectives and a lot of long, lonely, sleepless nights where he paced the home he'd expected to raise his family in, alone, had lifted from his chest. Freeing him to breathe, smile, walk with a spring in his step.

If only he hadn't forgotten how.

Loyal's pickup pulled in as Zane started for the back door of the feed mill. He stopped, waiting.

He wasn't sure how things were going to play out – how he was going to watch his daughters and work on his farm – and he was pretty sure he wasn't going to have much time to visit and socialize.

That's the reason he made sure to be here tonight, and the reason he waited now.

After all, it had been six weeks since he'd seen Loyal. After he and Madeline had had a hasty wedding, they'd flown out to Hollywood to tape the first eight episodes of their new show.

Unbelievable that Loyal was in front of cameras, taping a show in Hollywood. There could be no doubt what he and Madeline had was true love.

Zane couldn't help but be a little jealous – he'd love to find a woman who not only loved him, but who made him a better man. The idea seemed like a fairy tale. If he hadn't seen it happen to not just Loyal, but to Chandler and Clark, too, he would never believe it. Even Deacon seemed to be more with Blair beside him.

And they'd all, except Deacon, chosen poorly the first time.

Zane might think that there was hope yet for him, except he was the only one with four children. No woman in her right mind would take him on with his girls, too. And his girls came first. Now and forever.

"Hey, man! Good to see a real cowboy hat and boots that know how to work." Loyal had parked and walked over to where Zane waited, deep in thought.

"Thanks for telling me. Guess I'll stay in bed tomorrow morning and let my boots do the feeding." Zane grabbed Loyal's outstretched hand and drew him in for a back-slapping hug. Being the oldest brother in a house full of boys hadn't exactly helped him develop any kind of emotional depth, but he could admit he missed his brother.

His ex would lament his lack of emotional depth.

It might prove to be a problem with a house full of girls.

"I heard you got some good news while Madeline and I were gone."

"Sure did. They come next week." It was impossible to say that without grinning.

"Congratulations." Loyal gave his back one last slap before they turned and started walking toward the back door. "You hiring a housekeeper or a nanny or something?"

He'd thought about it, but really didn't want to. "I don't think so."

"You ever have all four girls by yourself before?" Loyal asked, scrunching his face up like he was trying to remember.

"A couple times." For one night. He tried not to grimace. It would probably be best to hire someone to help, but he'd sunk his available cash into a new tractor and baler, thinking he'd pick up some custom farming in the spring.

The last lawyer bill had been more than he was expecting and he was wiped out. He wasn't down to his last dime, but he needed to be

THE BEAST GETS HIS COWGIRL IN THE SHOW ME STATE

pretty frugal until summer when he could conceivably start expecting to make some money on baling hay.

"Guess you know what you're doing then," Loyal said, having no idea how inaccurate his oldest brother considered that statement.

He didn't have a flipping clue what he was doing. His one and only goal had been to get his kids away from his ex. She wasn't too bad when she was on her meds, but the last time she'd gone off them – last week – his daughters had been found barefoot in their nightgowns, crying in a graveyard. Apparently his ex had gotten them up in the middle of the night, dropped them off and driven away.

Hence the emergency court order granting him full custody. He'd have flown out to Arizona to get them himself, but it took a while to get everything sorted out. His lawyer had advised him to let the system work it out.

He still wasn't sure that was the best advice, but he'd followed it and now his girls were going to be his.

"Maybe you should just get married. Then you wouldn't have to worry about a housekeeper or nanny."

"Being stupid is how I got in this mess to begin with." He'd thought he was in love. Turned out he'd just been hoodwinked.

Speaking of, odds were pretty good his youngest daughter wasn't even his, but he'd never been able to love her less, nor even broach the subject of a paternity test. One look at those chubby little baby cheeks, that cute little bow mouth, those long baby fingers and that total and complete innocence and dependence, and he'd not been able to do anything but love her.

"Well, if you need any help, let me know." Loyal slapped his leg and grinned.

"You going back to Hollywood to tape more shows?"

"I don't think so. Think Madeline wants to try her hand at being a mom."

Zane narrowed his eyes. "You saying...?"

"Yep." Loyal didn't even try to contain the pride that lengthened his stride and kept his shoulders back.

"Congratulations," Zane said. "What does Patty think?"

"She's excited to be a big sister. She wants a brother."

"You put your order in?"

"We'll take what the Good Lord gives us. Happily."

Zane truly was happy for his brother.

Maybe, if he were really blessed, his daughters at least would find that kind of love. He'd had his chance. He'd chosen poorly, and now his biggest concern had to be raising his girls. If that meant selling his new tractor so he could afford to hire a nanny or housekeeper, then he supposed that's exactly what he'd do. No sacrifice was too big for his little girls.

THANK YOU SO MUCH FOR reading!

A Marriage of Convenience in the Show Me State is the next book in the series.

Reviews are welcome and appreciated.

Printed in Great Britain
by Amazon